The Flight of Icarus

By the same author
The Bark Tree

The Flight of Icarus

Raymond Queneau
translated by Barbara Wright

A New Directions Book

Originally published in French as *Le vol d'Icare*
© 1968 by Editions Gallimard. This translation,
under arrangement with them, was first published in the United States hardbound
(ISBN:0-8112-0482-0) and as New Directions
Paperbook 358 (ISBN:0-8112-0483-9) in 1973.

Manufactured in the United States of America

New Directions Books are published for James Laughlin
by New Directions Publishing Corporation
333 Sixth Avenue, New York 10014

TRANSLATOR'S NOTE

(Adapted from *Letter to Andrée Bergens*, published in the Queneau number of the French magazine, L'HERNE.)

You ask me some very simple, very clear questions about translating Queneau, and I will try to answer them equally simply and clearly.

Why I embarked on translating Queneau, and what difficulties he presents to the translator.

I started translating Queneau by accident, because I was lucky enough to be asked to translate two of his short stories. Having done so, I was hooked.

All translation, without exception, is difficult, and I am never quite sure why people imagine that Queneau is more difficult to translate than anyone else. Is it because of his puns? But many other writers make puns, and they are rarely such amusing ones as Queneau's. You'll notice that I don't say such *good* ones — because Queneau is, of course, the master of the intentionally awful pun. And the exercise of trying to match them in English is in itself amusing, and challenging, and on the occasions when one feels one has more or less succeeded, the satisfaction is great.

Or is Queneau considered difficult to translate because of his use of popular language? Pinget says of his own writing that his basic problem is to find a *tone*. It isn't until he has found the tone of the book he is hatching that he is able to go ahead and write it. The same applies to translation. The most important thing is to try and match

5

your author's tone, and the difficulty is only one of degree when that tone includes neologisms, original syntax, recondite allusions, popular language, etc.

The problem for the translator with the latter is, of course, that he has to invent, or use a synthesis of, an equivalent popular language which the reader will accept as modern, but which is not that of any particular English or American group – Cockney or Bronx, say. Queneau's characters are French, they live in a French environment, and they must stay there: to make them speak any specific English dialect would be to situate them where they don't belong. If you read, as I did in a recent translation, one French peasant supposedly saying of another: 'He would never set the Thames on fire', you are immediately jerked out of context, and out of your illusion. The man in the street takes it that when he reads a book in translation he is simply reading an exact replica of the original in a language he happens to understand. The ideal translation sustains him in this illusion.

With *The Flight of Icarus*, of course, there is no question of a 'modern' popular language. Here, the thing is to use a language that the modern reader can accept as being more or less that of Queneau's 1895 characters. Not forgetting, as always, the occasional flagrant anachronism that Queneau puts in to amuse himself (and us), as well as for other artistic reasons. 'How extremely Pirandellian', says Morcol, at the very beginning of the book.

Given that finding the appropriate 'tone' is the basic necessity for a translation, the difficulties must surely be less when the translator is in sympathy with the author. I hope I will not be thought presumptuous if I say that I feel that I am somewhere, somehow, on Queneau's wavelength – but this is why, in translating him, I think less of the difficulties and more of the fun and the (spiritual) reward.

Another point on difficulties: it is much less difficult to translate a good writer than a bad one: it is much less difficult to translate an author who has something to say, and who says it, than one who never seems to be quite sure what he *is* trying to say. When one has translated what we in England irreverently call 'French Art Critics' Prose', one can only, by comparison, consider Queneau simplicity itself. The translator is often, perhaps, the only person who really knows how a writer writes. He has to analyse everything *à fond*, strip all these pages of black marks on white paper down to their bare bones of semantics, overtones, undertones, euphony, rhythm, 'internal rhyme' — everything — and then try and recover the skeleton with new flesh and blood which nevertheless resembles the original so closely that it might be its twin brother. Now with Queneau, every word is there for a purpose — no other word could be substituted for it. Every phrase, every chapter he writes is there for a purpose and plays its precise, complicated part in the whole. In translating Queneau, there is always a solution waiting somewhere to be found, and all the translator has to do (all he has to do!) — is to find it. With some other writers, though, often there *can* be no real solution: where is the satisfaction, when something has originally been sloppily thought out and sloppily expressed, in finding the exact (sloppy) equivalent?

In what way is Queneau different from other writers?

I seem to have more or less answered this question above. There is also the fact that 'what he is writing' and 'what he is writing about' are the same thing. It is just beginning to be fashionable for people to say that nothing serious can be written without humour. Well, Queneau has always known that, and he has always put it into practice. It may be because his writing is such an intricate mixture of so many apparently disparate elements that one can read him again and again — and again — perhaps each time unconsciously approaching the Quenellian kaleidoscope from a different angle, but each time discovering something new.

How do I go about translating Queneau?
Every translator presumably finds a way of translating that suits himself, but which would not necessarily be valid for anyone else. However: first, I ask the publisher to give me plenty of time. Then I read the book several times, possibly making notes, either of difficulties or of spontaneous solutions. Then, first draft, longhand, in pencil, in an exercise book, with a separate notebook for queries of all sorts, as there are always some points on which I have to consult encyclopaedias or French friends. Often my French friends don't know the answers, and while this is very good for my ego, it obviously doesn't get me any further. There usually remain some irreducible points which defeat everyone and on which I have to consult Monsieur Queneau, though naturally I try to bother him as little as possible.

After I have gone over the first draft, I have it typed. Then I make further corrections on the typescript. With *Zazie*, I am amazed to remember that at this point I gave the typescript to three separate friends, all of whom knew Queneau's work well, and asked them for their comments. I suppose that I had the effrontery to do this because it was the first Queneau novel that I had translated, and I was scared. Nowadays I simply don't have the cheek, because I realise how much work is involved. But to get such opinions *at this stage*, is invaluable. In theory, of course, this sort of advice is the job of the publisher's reader but, in my experience, publishers either have practically nothing to say, or else argue over trifles, and press me to change things that I am sure are right. I reckon to know exactly why I have done whatever I have done, but to remain open to suggestions for improvements from someone who is seeing the work with a fresh eye.

A final confession. Quite often, when I am looking for some reference in one of my Queneau translations, I find myself reading on, as if I had never seen it before, and I feel quite pleased. But one Christmas, with a French friend, we tried an experiment. We read each other passages from my translation of *Zazie*, and then tried to translate it back into French. All we got was a very, *very* pale imitation of the original.

Icare, dixit, ubi es? Qua te regione requiram?

OVID

I

On the papers no sign of Icarus: between them – ditto.

He looks under the furniture, he opens the cupboards, he goes and looks in the privy: no Icarus.

So he takes his hat and stick, he's in the street, he hails a fly.

'Cabman, drive to number 47 rue Bochart de Saron, and don't spare the horses!'

The fly flies, in no time at all they're at number 47 rue Bochart de Saron. The fare gets out, says 'wait for me', dashes into the house, climbs up four floors, the door opens.

SURGET My dear fellow! What a pleasant surprise!

HUBERT None of your eburnean courtesies! After what you've done to me!

SURGET I? What?

HUBERT I have a bone to pick with you. Follow me.

He leads Surget into his own study, sits down in his place and rakes through the papers on the table.

SURGET Careful! don't make hay of my forthcoming novel!

HUBERT Come on! Admit it! Admit that he's here.

SURGET He? Who's *he*?

HUBERT (reading) Etienne was secretly in love with Victorine . . . blah blah blah . . . her hair was as yellow as ripe corn . . . blah blah blah . . . Georges, her fiancé, was a graduate of the Ecole Polytechnique . . . blah blah blah . . .

11

SURGET Nosey!

HUBERT (thoughtfully) He doesn't seem to be here.

SURGET He? Who's *he*?

HUBERT You remember, the other day, I read you the first few pages of my new book . . .

SURGET No reason to come and turn mine upside down!

HUBERT You were good enough to think highly of my chief character, though I had only barely begun to outline him. You complimented me on him.

SURGET Perhaps.

HUBERT He was called Icarus.

SURGET I remember.

HUBERT Well — he's disappeared!

SURGET He can't have! What a joke!

HUBERT It's no laughing matter. It would be an irreparable loss for me if I couldn't find him.

SURGET Yes, but you don't really think . . .

HUBERT It isn't a question of thinking, but of knowing. Where is he?

SURGET I've no idea.

HUBERT Swear it!

SURGET Yes, but you're not really going to suspect me of having stolen him from you, are you?

HUBERT That was precisely my unspoken thought.

SURGET But . . . zounds! You insult me: you offend me!

HUBERT Swear!

SURGET You can see for yourself . . . Etienne . . . Victorine . . .Georges . . .they've nothing in common with your Icarus. And then there are a Durand, a Duvel and a Dupont . . . and a concierge whom I call – and I must say, rather drolly, I think – Pipelet.

HUBERT You could have given him a pseudonym.

SURGET I detest that. I only recognise real names.

HUBERT And what if he were to adopt one, without your knowledge?

SURGET The identity of my characters is no mystery to me.

HUBERT And what about your flat? He may be hiding somewhere. I'm going to have a look.

He inspects the whole flat, opens the cupboards, looks under the furniture, goes and examines the privy.

HUBERT What luxury. A real English one, with water.

SURGET Thanks to a small legacy my wife came into. It costs the earth but, as the saying goes, money has no smell.

HUBERT And still no sign of Icarus.

SURGET So far as Icarus is concerned, I swear . . .

HUBERT What do you swear? And what are the oaths of a blackguard like you worth?

SURGET On my word of honour . . . As the saying goes: many a true word is a word of honour. And *honi soit qui mal y pense.*

HUBERT Your word of honour isn't enough.

SURGET Perhaps he's with one of our colleagues?

HUBERT You don't really expect me to traipse around to all our colleagues, do you?

SURGET Particularly as novelists are such liars.

HUBERT How true. Except you, of course. Then you swear?

SURGET On my honour, I swear that Icarus is not here — and I may add that I don't know where he is.

HUBERT I believe you, this time, but that doesn't get me any farther. What shall I do? What shall I do?

SURGET If I may be allowed to make a suggestion — why don't you engage a detective?

HUBERT Ridiculous idea. He won't understand a thing.

SURGET Don't you know Morcol — the Subtle Shadowing specialist? The man who follows adulterous women and finds lost sheep. He has appeared in many novels under different names. A second Vidocq. A second Lecoq. As the saying goes: there are times when it's ridiculous to fight against a shadow. He'll find your Icarus for you.

HUBERT I've no great confidence.

He goes to see him, all the same.

He stops at the door; an enamelled plate, *Morcol, Discretion, 2nd floor.* A venomously nauseating corridor leads to a similar type of staircase.

Hubert pulls a cord; a bell rings.

MORCOL Monsieur: I am at your disposition.

HUBERT Mine is a very unusual case.

MORCOL All my cases are unusual, Monsieur.

HUBERT Mine is very particularly so.

MORCOL That is for me to judge.

HUBERT I hesitate ... because it is such a strange business ...

MORCOL I hear the most widely varied stories.

14

HUBERT Well then. Let me introduce myself: Hubert Lubert, a novelist by profession, by vocation, even, and I might add, of some renown. Since I am a novelist, then, I write novels. And since I write novels, I deal with characters. And now one of them has vanished. Literally. A novel I had just begun, about ten pages, fifteen at the most, and in which I had placed the highest hopes, and now the principal character, whom I had barely begun to outline, disappears. As I obviously cannot continue without him, I have come to ask you to find him for me.

MORCOL (dreamily) How extremely Pirandellian.

HUBERT Pirandellian?

MORCOL An adjective derived from Pirandello. It's true, though; you couldn't understand.

HUBERT A client?

MORCOL Ssh! Let's get back to the point. What did your fellow look like?

HUBERT Difficult to say. I had only a rather sketchy knowledge of him. Ten or fifteen pages, you understand, I hadn't got any farther than the exposition . . .

MORCOL The *Exposition Universelle*? The Universal Exhibition?

HUBERT That is not foreign to my theme, but I was in fact referring to the exposition of my subject matter. The modern novel, as you are aware, does not begin by exhibiting the principal character, it leads up to him gradually . . .

MORCOL All right, all right. Obviously you haven't got a photograph.

HUBERT Obviously not.

MORCOL Allow me to ask you a few questions. Age?

HUBERT Young, as I saw him.

15

MORCOL Can't you be more precise?

HUBERT Let's say about twenty.

MORCOL (ironically) You aren't one of those people who like to compete with the Registrar General?

HUBERT That is indeed not my style.

MORCOL Let's get on to his physical characteristics, then. Height?

HUBERT One metre seventy-six centimetres precisely.

MORCOL But you do compete with the metric system?

HUBERT Ha. ha.

MORCOL Let us continue. Nose?

HUBERT Straight, no doubt.

MORCOL Hair?

HUBERT Dark brown, I think.

MORCOL Special peculiarities?

HUBERT I haven't given him any.

MORCOL Residence?

HUBERT I intended him to live in the rue Bleue.

MORCOL What number?

HUBERT An odd number.

MORCOL Which one? There are quite a lot.

HUBERT I haven't decided yet.

MORCOL None of this helps me very much.

HUBERT As I told you, I'd only just begun him.

MORCOL Has he any relations? Any friends?

HUBERT I haven't thought about that yet, but I have a very pure fiancée in mind for him.

MORCOL Does he like her?

HUBERT We haven't reached that point yet.

MORCOL Have you perhaps had some disagreement?

HUBERT I don't think so. I am preparing a melancholy existence for him which could hardly displease him because he knows no other. I want him to like moonlight, fairy roses, the exotic types of nostalgia, the languors of Spring, fin-de-siècle neuroses — all things that I personally abhor, but which go down well in the present-day novel.

MORCOL Perhaps he hates all that, too.

HUBERT He doesn't know anything about it.

MORCOL He may have some inkling . . .

HUBERT You worry me.

MORCOL I imagine that your bird has flown.

HUBERT There's certainly a fly in the ointment somewhere. Don't you think it's more likely that he's been stolen?

MORCOL I shall start with the flight-hypothesis, and with an advance of ten louis.

HUBERT The deuce.

MORCOL You are hardly making things easy for me. Your data are extremely vague . . .

HUBERT I'm doing my best. Here — take these ten louis, and see that you find him soon. I shan't be able to write a word until the mystery's solved and Icarus comes back.

MORCOL I acknowledge receipt of the ten louis; I'll make a note of his name.

He writes Dicky Ruscombe in his notebook while Lubert hands him his card. Morcol is to let him know the moment he has the slightest lead. He takes his departure, while Morcol reflects.

MORCOL Less than nothing, the clues this gentleman has given me, and I am supposed to do something with this less than nothing. I must work out what method to use in this particular case. I have several strings to my bow but the first that comes to hand is that of argument by analogy. Supposing that I were this Dicky Ruscombe who lives in the rue Bleue and that I had taken to flight. I shouldn't go back to the rue Bleue. Where would I go? As I shouldn't have much experience of life, being only some ten or fifteen pages old, I should naively go to a street with an analagous name. Not knowing Paris very well, I should find myself in the rue Blanche. This is a line of argument which I consider impeccable.

He goes out, dressed in his grey paletot and universal top-hat.

MORCOL To the rue Blanche!

II

At the Globe and Two Worlds Tavern in the rue Blanche there was only one free table, which seemed to be waiting for Icarus. It was in fact waiting for him. Icarus sat down, a slow but sure waiter came and asked him what he wished to partake of. Icarus didn't know. He looked at the nearby tables; their occupants were drinking absinthe. He pointed to that milky liquid, believing it to be harmless. In the glass he was brought, the beverage appeared to be green; Icarus might well have thought this an optical illusion had he known what an optical illusion was; he was also brought a strangely shaped spoon, a lump of sugar and a carafe of water.

Icarus pours the water on the absinthe, which assumes the colour of milt. Exclamations from the neighbouring tables.

FIRST DRINKER Disgraceful! it's a massacre!

SECOND DRINKER The fellow's never drunk absinthe in his life!

FIRST DRINKER Vandalism! Pure vandalism!

SECOND DRINKER Let's be indulgent; let's simply call it ignorance.

FIRST DRINKER (to Icarus) My young friend, have you never drunk absinthe before?

ICARUS Never, Monsieur. I didn't even know that it was called absinthe.

SECOND DRINKER Where've you come from, then?

19

ICARUS Er . . .

FIRST DRINKER What does it matter! My young friend, I'm going to teach you to prepare a glass of absinthe.

ICARUS Thank you, Monsieur.

FIRST DRINKER In the first place, do you know what absinthe is?

ICARUS No, Monsieur.

FIRST DRINKER She is our comforter, alas, our consolation, she is our only hope, she is our aim, our goad, and like an elixir — which she is, of course — the source of our elation, it is she who lends us strength to reach the end of the road.

SECOND DRINKER What's more, she is an angel whose magnetic fingers hold the gifts of blessed sleep, of ecstatic dreams untold.

FIRST DRINKER Kindly don't interrupt me, Monsieur. That is precisely what I was about to say and, I may add, with the poet: she is the glory of the Gods, the mystic crock of gold.

ICARUS I'd never dare drink that.

FIRST DRINKER Not that, no! You've ruined it by slopping all that tap-water over it in such barbaric fashion! Never! (to the waiter) Bring Monsieur another absinthe.

The waiter brings another absinthe. Icarus stretches his hand out towards his glass.

FIRST DRINKER Stop, idiot! (Icarus rapidly withdraws his hand). You don't drink it like that! I'll show you. You place the spoon on the glass in which the absinthe already reposes, and then you put a lump of sugar on the aforementioned spoon, whose singular shape will not have escaped your notice. Then, very slowly, you pour the water over the sugar lump, which will start to dissolve

20

and, drop by drop a fecundating and sacchariferous rain will fall into the elixir and cause it to become cloudy. Once again you pour on a little water which beads, and beads, and so on, until the sugar has dissolved, but the elixir has not acquired too aqueous a consistency. Observe it, my young friend, watch the operation taking effect . . . an inconceivable alchemy . . .

ICARUS Isn't it pretty?

He stretches his hand out towards his glass.

THIRD DRINKER And now pour the contents on the floor.

THE TWO OTHERS Blasphemy!

THIRD DRINKER It's poison.

ENSEMBLE OF DRINKERS Blasphemy!

CHORUS OF WAITERS Blasphemy!

THE PROPRIETOR Hell and damnation!

ICARUS (bewildered) What am I to do?

ALL MINUS ONE Drink it!

THIRD DRINKER Don't drink it!

Ter, quater, quinquies . . .

This continues until the door of the tavern opens and a young woman comes in.

CHORUS OF DRINKERS (FIRST HALF) LN! You couldn't have come at a better time.

CHORUS OF DRINKERS (SECOND HALF) LN! She couldn't have come at a better time.

FIRST HALF OF THE CHORUS You shall be the judge!

SECOND HALF You shall be the arbiter!

21

FIRST HALF You shall be our Solomon!

SECOND HALF You shall be our Balkis!

LN What's going on?

THIRD DRINKER I don't see why this whore . . .

LN That's what I am, and I'm proud of it. Whore I am and whore I remain. But why a judge, an arbiter, a Solomon?

FIRST DRINKER Come over here. Look at this young man.

LN Isn't he handsome!

SECOND DRINKER Should he drink his absinthe?

THIRD DRINKER Or shouldn't he? But I don't see why this whore . . .

ICARUS Mademoiselle . . .

LN Monsieur.

ICARUS I shall do what you tell me to do, Mademoiselle.

THIRD DRINKER So young, and already a lost soul . . . Absinthism and grisette . . .

He disappears abruptly.

LN (sitting down at the table of one of the other customers and indicating Icarus)
Who is he?

FIRST DRINKER I don't know him, and you can see he's not an habitué. Just a beginner. He didn't even know how to prepare his absinthe . . .

CHORUS OF DRINKERS Well! Shall he drink it or shan't he?

LN (to Icarus). Drink it, young man!

ICARUS (wets his lips and makes a grimace).

22

FIRST DRINKER Nothing seek, nothing find. Try again.

SECOND DRINKER Go on, try again.

ICARUS (putting down his glass). I shall only try it again if Mademoiselle tells me to.

LN Mademoiselle does tell you to. Have another sip.

Icarus drinks a mouthful. He smiles politely, and then imbibes another mouthful.

SECOND DRINKER Well, what do you think of it?

ICARUS (after a third, a fourth, a fifth mouthful, pensively).
How far away my nurse's milk seems . . . how the heavenly bodies are increasing and multiplying . . . how the night fades into the pale nebulae. It is already blue, the opalescent sea is hushed . . . how far away I seem from all that . . . in the vicinity of the star called Absinthe . . .

FIRST DRINKER Drunk already!

LN (moving over to Icarus's table) Well, pet, is it good?

ICARUS I don't know whether it's good or not, but I do wonder what people would say if they saw me under the influence of this drink.

LN But they do see you. We all do. And it doesn't particularly surprise us.

ICARUS Just as well.

LN It's odd, but you make me feel shy.

ICARUS I'm certainly shyer than you, Mademoiselle. I'm not used to the world — the great world — and this is the first time I've been out on my own.

LN Were you at boarding-school?

ICARUS My goodness no.

LN In prison?

ICARUS Not that, either.

LN Tell all.

ICARUS The stove is unlit, for spring is here. The ink flows on the white paper in shallow, fertile rivulets from which friends, relations and enemies are born, as well as indoor plants, in the corners of apartments furnished with rep and velvet, mahogany and Cordova leather. The quill conducts a little world of objects and names towards a destiny which escapes me. I am standing in the middle of all this, near an armchair, and waiting. Every so often, I move. I watch the housekeeper bring in the Mocha coffee or the English tea. Madame de Champvaux calls at five o'clock; I have never seen her, he shuts me in at this moment, I hear them going into the adjoining bedroom, and then I hear no more. The apartment is extremely sound-proof. At other times, various gentlemen come and chat; their cigars, with lengthening ash and chewed-up end, burn down in the ashtrays. I still can't really properly see the people round me . . . a girl, perhaps . . . her father . . . The winter's over, spring is here . . .

FIRST DRINKER All of which is of no great interest.

ICARUS That's exactly what I think. My humble self, as I am well aware, is not of the slightest interest.

LN Nonsense, pet, nonsense. You don't want to take any notice of the general opinion of every lo . . .

FIRST DRINKER Me? Low!

LN (imperturbably) . . . of every locality you happen to be in.

FIRST DRINKER Ha ha! Well, I'll stand another round.

SECOND DRINKER Me too.

LN Be reasonable. You'll make the young man ill.

ICARUS But I'm quite all right; my head feels hot and my liver feels cold, which at the moment isn't at all unpleasant.

FIRST DRINKER You see! Waiter, another round!

ICARUS I don't know how to thank you.

LN You can thank him later.

SECOND DRINKER He must be able to appreciate the third round.

LN (to Icarus). Will you be able to hold out until then?

ICARUS I'm floating a little.

The third round is brought.

FIRST DRINKER (observing Icarus preparing his absinthe). Not too bad. He's improving.

SECOND DRINKER He still pours the water rather too quickly.

LN You're always criticising! (to Icarus). A very good beginning, pet.

MORCOL (entering). (to Morcol). This is the third tavern in the rue Blanche that I have visited. Which of these customers could possibly be Dicky Ruscombe? (to the waiter). Waiter, have you by any chance seen a young man one metre 76 tall, with dark brown hair, a straight nose . . .

WAITER Have a look over there.

MORCOL There does seem to be some resemblance . . . but he's probably more like one metre 77. Never mind, let's go and see, anyway.

He goes over to Icarus's table.

MORCOL Monsieur, excuse me if I excuse myself, but I have a message for Monsieur Dicky Ruscombe. You are not, by any chance, he?

ICARUS No, Monsieur. Thus am I nowise nempned.

MORCOL Are you quite sure?

ICARUS Even though I am beginning to take wing under the influence of a strong drink, I can be quite categorical that that is not my name.

MORCOL I not only have a message for Monsieur Dicky Ruscombe, but also a considerable sum of money for him. A very considerable sum. Are you quite sure that you do not bear that name?

ICARUS Absolutely certain.

MORCOL In that case, Monsieur, I will withdraw.

In the street.

MORCOL The lure of easy money: an infallible trap. So he wasn't Dicky Ruscombe, then. And yet he must have been one metre 77. Let us continue to pursue our enquiries from tavern to tavern.

III

LN You were quite right to deny it. It was a trap.

ICARUS The fact is that my name isn't Ruscombe.

LN And what *is* your name?

ICARUS I'm not very sure any more . . . I've stopped soaring, I'm swimming, now . . . in deep water. And you, Mademoiselle: Hélène?

LN No, LN in two letters. I am of cruciverbal origin.

ICARUS Cruciverbal?

LN It's true, you couldn't understand. Aren't you hungry?

ICARUS Indeed I am, since this thing I'm drinking is called an aperitif.

LN Then we'll go and have dinner. Are you going to invite me?

ICARUS I'll have to see how much money I have, first.

WAITER And, even before that, pay for your drinks.

ICARUS (spreads out some small change on the table). Here you are.

WAITER (picks up 75 centimes, under LN's watchful eye).

LN (stands up. To the people at the nearby tables) Messieurs.

FIRST DRINKER I hope you are not dissatisfied with your first experience?

27

ICARUS Delighted, but all this disturbs me a little, and I have a feeling that I'm eluding the forces of gravitation. Messieurs . . .

He bows to them and goes out, followed by LN.

In the street.

ICARUS And now, how are we going to manage to eat?

LN We'll go to a little place I know where you can eat for 1 franc 50. Don't worry. I shan't ruin you.

ICARUS Come on, then. I'd like another absinthe.

LN laughs.

In the restaurant.

WAITER (a different one). What a pleasure! Please sit down.

Icarus sits down, so does LN, next to him. She picks up the menu with determination.

They eat.
Icarus pays and they leave.
Her room.

LN How d'you like my place?

ICARUS Nice. I can't think of any other word: nice.

They kiss.

Later:

LN I still don't know much about you.

ICARUS I can tell you that I was born about 1875, under the principate of MacMahon. I was about fourteen at the time of the Universal Exhibition. At least, I think I was. I was probably living in the provinces, my father was a blacksmith — or possibly a locksmith. He took me to see the marvels of the terminating century. This admirable exhibition covered a surface of 958,572 square metres and

28

it was estimated that it was visited by 33 million people. I was one of these 33 million visitors perambulating the 958,572 square metres of its surface. My father was particularly anxious for me to visit the Hall of Machines, which was no less than 450 metres long, 115 wide and 45 high, and also the 300 metre-high Tower designed by an engineer called Eiffel and made entirely of iron, not forgetting the luminous Fountains designed by an engineer of the name of Bechmann. We paid great attention to the products of the 55,486 industrial exhibitors, and looked somewhat more rapidly at the works of the 5,110 Beaux-Arts exhibitors. Then Monsieur Lubert crossed it all out.

LN Monsieur Lubert?

ICARUS He baptised me, and I was living quietly in his apartment waiting to fulfil the destiny he was weaving for me. One day he forgot to close his manuscript . . .

LN His manuscript?

ICARUS Yes. And a gust of wind came and carried me off. Instead of returning to that graphic domicile I continued on my way until I found myself in the street. Then I began to wonder what to do, where to go, and then by accident, attracted by the odour of what I now know to be absinthe, I went into the tavern where I made your acquaintance, Mademoiselle.

LN You can call me LN, you know.

ICARUS But none of this tells me what is going to become of me now. As you see, LN, I haven't much experience of life, but I am not unaware of the fact that people have to eat and sleep somewhere where they are safe from the wolves and the storm, nor that, to be able to eat and sleep somewhere safe from the wolves and the storm, you have to have a lot of money and I haven't any or at least I have very little or more precisely I have hardly any.

29

LN Don't worry, I'll see you get something to eat every day, and you can sleep in this place — my room.

ICARUS But what about all the money?

LN That's no problem — I shall earn enough for two.

ICARUS Really? That would be wonderful.

LN It would, wouldn't it, my love?

ICARUS Then you'll be my piggy bank. But how will you do it?

LN Don't bother your head about that. I'll see that you have enough to eat, and that you have a roof over your head.

ICARUS It's all too beautiful . . . providing that Monsieur Lubert doesn't discover me.

LN Be on your guard! Be on your guard!

ICARUS But how?

LN By being on your guard.

IV

MORCOL (coming out of the seventh tavern in the rue Blanche, having drunk the same number of absinthes).

Another f****** fiasco! However hard I Run about the Streets, Scour the Countryside and Plough through the Waves, I'm still up a gum-tree. However hard I live it up, I'll still have to give up. It's like looking for a camel in a sieve. And yet I'm using all my reasoning powers . . . I'm reasoning . . . and, as the saying goes, reason rules all things. But here there seems to be rhyme without reason. It may rhyme but it accordeth not. What can I do, though? Miaow at the moon? Spit on my feet? Gnaw my teeth? These are all procedures which are infallibly fallible when it comes to solving a problem, and ones that have never figured among the methods I am in the habit of employing. I shall reject them with a flip of the finger — and let's start by liberating our spirits from the noxious effluvia we have just been ingurgitating.

Which he does.

And now let us consider things clearly, and in the first place let us dismiss the flight-hypothesis. With such a fledgling there can be no question of anything other than a brief escapade; he wouldn't be able to go far, which means that he couldn't have gone beyond the rue Blanche. He wouldn't have dared venture into any other district. Must we come back to the idea of theft, then? or of kidnapping? but who would be interested in such a colourless character, one wonders, except a colleague. A colleague who's got stuck, and is looking for characters for his novel. My client must have been right.

A VOICE IN THE FOG Coming, darling?

MORCOL Oh, oh? Whisper who dares?

A VOICE IN THE FOG Don't be afraid, my popsy-copsy.

MORCOL Does this anonymous person think he's being funny?

LN (appearing under the light of a street lamp: her shadow is projected along the pavement and extends into the distance). I repeat, my handsome, what I have just said: are you coming?

MORCOL What for? (to Morcol). In any case it isn't a he, it's a she.

LN What for? that's a good one. You wouldn't be a virgin at your age, would you? (she recognises him). Hell!

MORCOL I have a feeling, Mademoiselle, that I've met you before somewhere.

LN There's no mystery about it. At the Globe and Two Worlds Tavern, where I was having an absinthe with a friend.

MORCOL Ah yes. The young man who was one metre 77 tall and who wasn't called Dicky Ruscombe.

LN That's right.

MORCOL And this Dicky Ruscombe — he wouldn't by any chance be one of your customers, would he?

LN I don't know anyone of that name.

MORCOL (to Morcol). One more reason to think that it isn't a flight, but a theft.

LN So?

MORCOL So nothing. Good-bye Mademoiselle. I shall continue my enquiry.

LN What about the time you've made me waste? I demand compensation.

MORCOL That's logical, since Mademoiselle is on the

beat.

LN I'm the drummer of Arcole.

She beats him gently on the stomach: it reverberates.

MORCOL Search me from top to toe – you will find nothing but Reason. Here – here's a franc.

LN That'll come in handy for my piggy-bank.

MORCOL (alone in the street).

Just an insignificant incident.
Let us resume our argument at the point where I left it. It can only be a colleague.

He rings at Lubert's door.

HUBERT Who is it?

MORCOL The detective.

Hubert opens the door.

HUBERT Already? Have you found him?

MORCOL Not yet. Keep calm, keep calm.

HUBERT I'm dying with impatience.

MORCOL Die by all means but keep calm. My intellectual powers have caused me to change my mind. It can only be a theft. We cannot entirely reject the hypothesis that it is one of your colleagues, but I am also considering your various acquaintances. I want you to give me the names and addresses of all the people to whom you are linked by any sort of tie, of blood, of hostility, but in particular of friendship.

Lubert does so.
Morcol goes out.

HUBERT (alone). I didn't put Mme de Champvaux's name on the list. I am a man of honour.

V

Icarus was walking along the embankment, he was looking at the bookstalls but he didn't dare touch the old books because he didn't like dust and anyway the booksellers seemed to him to be frightening characters, Cerberuses defending their property rather than pleasant presenters of spiritual nourishment. They would reprimand you for no reason at all. He was reading the titles from a distance, under the shade of the chestnut trees. He was near the Quai de Gesvres when one of the titles attracted his attention. Four words which in all innocence seduced him: The Principles of Mechanics. After much hesitation, he addressed the dealer in these terms:

'Monsieur, excuse me, pardon me, but please may I touch this book?'

BOOKSELLER By all means, young man. Make yourself at home.

ICARUS You aren't being ironical? or joking? Making fun of me?

BOOKSELLER You can read me like an open book. Carry on!

ICARUS I dare not.

BOOKSELLER Here! — I'll help you.

He gets up from his camp stool, picks up the book and holds it out to Icarus.

BOOKSELLER It's pretty heavy-going.

ICARUS May I really open it?

BOOKSELLER Carry on, young man, consult it, inspect

34

it, you won't wear it out!

ICARUS Oh, thank you, Monsieur.

BOOKSELLER Are you interested in mechanics?

ICARUS No, Monsieur, not very much, I don't understand the first thing about it.

BOOKSELLER (taking the book out of his hands). With a bit of effort you're sure to understand *something*. Look — there are two volumes bound together: Vol. I consists of Pure Kinematics and Theoretical Mechanics, and Vol. II deals with the Mechanics of Bodies. It's a bargain.

ICARUS And is this book for sale?

BOOKSELLER Fifty centimes. A real bargain.

ICARUS The whole of my pocket money!

BOOKSELLER Come come, young man, this is a sacrifice you'll never regret. This book will teach you that all movements that are produced in the universe, whether with the co-operation of our will or independent of it, are due to forces which are exercised on the molecules of natural bodies and which change according to their natural divisions. These variations in distance are manifested in the life of animals and vegetables, and in explosions, detonations, the firing of projectiles, etc. You'll find all this on p. 242.

ICARUS Couldn't we put up a screen, though, between animal life and the firing of projectiles?

BOOKSELLER Just read what's written in this book. Fifty centimes, its a gift.

ICARUS Here you are, Monsieur.

He walks off, turning over the pages of the book.

ICARUS The equilibrium of an obstructed solid body . . . interesting . . . and even rather sad . . .

VI

Doctor Lajoie prescribes a little herb tea after dinner and a light but not too strict diet.

'No chestnut purée then?' asks the sufferer.

'No chestnut purée'.

'You're depriving me of everything good in life,' says the sick man.

'Very well then, I'll allow you to console yourself with truffles on Sundays and a small cup of coffee after every meal. That'll be two francs.'

After pocketing the two francs and ejecting the valetudinarian, Doctor Lajoie went into his waiting room to see if there was anyone there. Doctor Lajoie was the anxious type, the sort of man who always has the feeling that he hasn't posted his letter, and who checks seven times that he really has bolted the door. He knew perfectly well that no one else was waiting for him in the room set aside for that purpose, yet he had to make quite sure before he shut up shop and went to dine at his club, for he was a bachelor, and his housekeeper who usually opened the door to his patients had gone off to consult a healer in the provinces.

He goes into the waiting room then, and there, to his great, to his very great surprise, he finds someone. The someone and he look at each other in silence. Finally the Doctor says, in a voice that betrays some emotion:

'Come in, Sir'.

Why he said Sir he has no idea, he has not the slightest proof of the britannicity of the anonymous individual, but the latter does not seem surprised by this denomination.

He comes in.

'Sit down . . . Sir', says the Doctor.
He sits down.
Silence.

DOCTOR What are you suffering from, Sir?

SIR Everything.

DOCTOR And yet you are mobile. You are even very subtly mobile. If I am not being indiscreet, how did you get in? I'd shut the door.

SIR (taking a bunch of keys out of his pocket). By means of my stethometer.

DOCTOR Ah. (a pause). Well, I'll listen to your chest. Take your clothes off.

SIR I never take my clothes off. I'll tell you what I've got: whin in the scrotum, whining noises in the stomach, parpens in the pancreas . . .

DOCTOR (interrupting him) I see what it is. I'll give you a prescription (he writes it as he speaks). One gramme of bicarbonate of soda every day on rising in a glass of water with a little sugar in it. Here. That'll be two francs.

SIR (not understanding) Bicarbonate of soda?

DOCTOR It's a miracle medicine that has just been invented.

SIR Have many of your patients taken it? Because, personally you know, I'm rather wary.

DOCTOR More than a hundred! And always with excellent results.

SIR You have a great many patients, I see. Many from this neighbourhood?

DOCTOR I know all the writers and journalists who live round here and, I may add, all their lady friends. Not that I want to boast.

SIR Is Monsieur Lubert a patient of yours? The novelist?

DOCTOR Professional secrets . . .

SIR I'm not being indiscreet: it was he who gave me your name.

DOCTOR I am obliged to him.

SIR And amongst his circle of intimates . . .

DOCTOR What — *more* questions to ask me? If I understand aright, you're a false patient.

SIR You do understand aright.

DOCTOR And a false Sir?

SIR You understand even better.

DOCTOR Might you be an adventurer?

SIR Your understanding falters.

DOCTOR A sociologist, then? a follower of Le Play, conducting an enquiry?

SIR Don't let's go off at a tangent. Let's just suppose that I am no one.

DOCTOR Monsieur Outis (to Doctor Lajoie). I am ultra-cultured.

SIR Let us suppose that we are talking quietly among friends, that there are therefore no professional secrets to be considered; I ask a trivial question, quite casually, incidentally, and you answer trivially, quite casually, incidentally.

DOCTOR If I agree.

SIR Among your respected patients, is there a certain Dicky Ruscombe?

DOCTOR An Englishman? I haven't any. Not even you.

SIR My Dick isn't English. He's French. Ah yes, that's a

question I forgot to ask him. But does he know it himself? In any case, he's one metre 76 tall, has straight hair, a dark brown nose, and what colour eyes . . .

DOCTOR Your remarks, false Sir, are beginning to take on a certain mixed aspect. Might you not be suffering from slight mental confusion?

SIR The question that you incite me to ask myself causes me sincere anxiety. I'd never thought of it. Is Dick French or isn't he, that is the question.

DOCTOR As we say in French: voilà le hic.

SIR Not the hic, the Dick.

DOCTOR So you're looking for this man. And why?

SIR Let us drop the mask. I am Morcol, observation and discretion. At your service.

DOCTOR *I'm* not looking for anyone.

MORCOL Doctor, you are the physician of the famous novelist, Hubert Lubert. And he's suffering.

DOCTOR I've never prescribed anything other than herb tea for him.

MORCOL For reasons of which I am unaware, no doubt because you considered that the work he has undertaken is injurious to his health, to prevent him from continuing it you have dicknapped the principal character of his novel.

DOCTOR (stupefied by this neologism) Dicknapped?

MORCOL Well, kidnapped, if you like.

DOCTOR I! kidnap! commit a crime! You're barmy, Monsieur Morwhat?

MORCOL Morcol. Observation and discretion. At your service.

DOCTOR Don't need your service. And as to the dicknapping, I indignantly reject such a hypothesis.

39

MORCOL Let me search your papers — and your apartment.

DOCTOR You're barmy, I repeat. That's quite clear. You need treatment.

MORCOL Again! I'm ill and I don't know it, would that be it?

DOCTOR Since you don't want any bicarbonate of soda, lie down on that couch and tell me everything that comes into your head; it'll do you good.

MORCOL And will that help me to find my Dick?

DOCTOR At least it will help you to find Morcol again.

MORCOL Just by telling you what comes into my head?

DOCTOR Precisely.

MORCOL What? Something like flèche d'or fish neither nor murder most foul?

DOCTOR Yes. The method of Free Association.

MORCOL As you will have observed, I am not ignorant of it; it's a sort of moral search, wouldn't you say?

DOCTOR Ingenious.

MORCOL Well! I'm going to carry out a physical one.

Morcol goes through the apartment, shakes books, moves papers. The Doctor prudently allows him to get on with it.

DOCTOR (to Doctor Lajoie) A very sick man.

MORCOL Excuse me if I excuse myself, but Dicky Ruscombe is not in fact here. We'll go and look elsewhere: thank you, Doctor.

He goes out.

DOCTOR A very sick man.

40

VII

Icarus is waiting for LN, smoking a partagas and drinking port wine.

ICARUS I can only congratulate myself on having escaped from my originator's pages. What can he be doing without me, I wonder. Has he found someone to replace me? Hardly likely, because I'm pretty sure that I'm irreplaceable. No, he must be at a loss. He's looking for me, he's searching for me, that's certain, that fellow the other day at the tavern was in his pay. LN told me so and she knows a lot of things. But he'll never find me here. Hubert must have thought that I wouldn't be able to do without him, that I wouldn't be able to manage, and here I am with my board and lodging and all the rest. I can await the absence of events peacefully, and go on reading this book on theoretical mechanics of which I understand precisely nothing.

LN (coming back from her beat) My pet, I've brought you the result of a day's labour: some brawn, some Russian salad, a litre of red wine, and twelve francs fifty-four centimes. I was forgetting: some oranges and cakes from the patisserie on the corner: a cherry tart for you, a cream puff for me and an almond cake to share between us. I love you and you'll be happy.

ICARUS I am in fact happy; I've been rescued from my originator and I'm as free as the air (though I've learnt that even so it does have a little weight), I'm dreaming, and I'm going to have some brawn.

LN Let's eat!

They eat.

LN I'm going back to work and tonight we'll have supper at the Café Anglais.

ICARUS Am I well-enough dressed?

LN At the moment you're quite naked. I'll send you the tailor.

VIII

A Club. Club armchairs. Conversation.

JACQUES It seems that Goncourt has left his fortune — his considerable fortune — to found a prize to reward the best work of imagination of the year.

JEAN What does money matter: glory is enough for us.

JACQUES Oh! glory . . . I sometimes perceive its distant effluvia when my nose approaches the window of my ivory tower . . . distant effluvia . . . distant . . .

JEAN Posterity is on your side.

JACQUES I shall be read half a century hence, not before.

JEAN I shall be famous in my lifetime, and you when you are dead.

JACQUES Just between ourselves, and seeing that there aren't any journalists listening, I sometimes say to myself that posterity is a long way off. Even so, though, posterity is still posterity, it's not nothing.

JEAN Pah! That's just what it is, posterity — nothingness. Personally I like to anticipate my glory. What do I care if my name figures in a History of French Literature by some future Brunetière. I'd rather have a favourable review by Jules Lemaître or Anatole France.

JACQUES In short, de gustibus . . .

JEAN Non est discutandum. Let's forget about our different points of view which, after all, are only of purely subjective value – if they are of any value at all, that is – and tell me, my dear Jacques, how you are getting on with your work.

JACQUES Well, I'm still writing my novel.

JEAN What is it about? You did tell me something about it the other day, but in a somewhat obscure fashion.

JACQUES It isn't about anything.

JEAN Not about anything! That's most surprising.

JACQUES I wanted to give the impression of the colour mauve.

JEAN Go on, you not only surprise me, you interest me.

JACQUES If I had chosen to give the impression of the colour violet, I should have written a novel about ecclesiastical circles. For example, an ambitious priest with his eye on a bishopric, perhaps even on the papacy. He's hoping to become the first French sovereign pontiff.

JEAN Who's dressed in white, not in violet.

JACQUES That's why I gave up the idea. Or else I would have written about a geologist who had specialised in the study of amethysts; or a botanist who was an expert on aubergines.

JEAN But mauve?

JACQUES In the first place it's a modern colour, and that's what I want to be – modern.

JEAN How do you mean, a modern colour?

JACQUES It doesn't appear in the Littré dictionary: all it gives is the noun which refers either to a plant – the mallow – or to a dialect word for a sea-gull.

JEAN It's true that it isn't often employed as an adjective. And how do you see it, this modern colour?

JACQUES A very pale violet.

JEAN There aren't many objects of that colour, either natural or artificial.

JACQUES The sky, sometimes, when there's a storm brewing, or when the twilight is preparing to extinguish the sun. That's why I am writing an aerial, not to say celestial, novel.

JEAN But won't there be anything else in it but mauve?

JACQUES Adultery.

JEAN Adultery! If ever a subject has been done to death, if I may say so, that one has. In any case, all we novelists of the declining century write about adultery. It's beginning to get boring. That's all I ever do! You disappoint me. And you have your eye on posterity? You ought to choose something less fin-de-siècle.

JACQUES Yes, but the adultery will be mauve.

JEAN That's out of the ordinary.

JACQUES I certainly hope so.

JEAN And have you got all your dramatis personae together? The husband? The wife? The lover?

JACQUES Of course. The husband is the ironmaster, Polydore de Roubézieux, the wife's Christian name is Vitalie, née Dupont, but of the baronial family of that name. And the lover is the very young Adalbert de Chamissac-Piéplu. When I say lover, I mean future lover, because nothing has happened so far.

JEAN And this Chamissac-Piéplu, how long is it since you started him?

JACQUES Forty-eight hours.

JEAN How do you imagine him?

JACQUES One metre 76, dark brown hair, straight

45

nose. And his eyes, naturally, are mauve.

HUBERT (from the depths of a nearby armchair where he has heard the whole conversation). Not the slightest doubt, he's the thief. I must tell Morcol. Even though Icarus's eyes aren't mauve.

JEAN (to Jacques) And where does he live?

JACQUES That's obvious. Can't you guess?

JEAN Rue Bleue.

IX

Icarus is waiting for LN, smoking a partagas and drinking port wine. He is looking at a number of *L'Illustration*. The bell rings. He goes and opens the door.

THE VISITOR I can see you need me. I'm the tailor.

ICARUS Did LN send you?

TAILOR Mademoiselle LN did in fact ask me to call. I was advised of the state you are in. And in any case, I am not alone.

Enter

THE SHIRTMAKER
THE BOOTMAKER
THE HABERDASHER
THE HATTER
THE STICK AND UMBRELLA MERCHANT

They are all carrying cardboard boxes.

ICARUS So many people just to dress me!

TAILOR You're starting from scratch. (Directing the operations). Every morning we start from scratch. To dress a man is to dress a world. We start with the feet: here are the socks. For your legs, some underpants, a shirt for your torso, a collar for the neck, and don't forget the cuffs. And then we start again: shoes, trousers, braces, waistcoat, tie, jacket, hat. And a stick or a cane. Now you are equipped to face the great world. A greatcoat for the winter, a bum-freezer for mid-season.

TAILOR (withdrawing with his troupe). We were given a worm, and we turned it into a lion.

47

X

Jacques's apartment. He is smoking a partagas and drinking a glass of port wine. On the right, on his desk, the meticulously tidy pages of his forthcoming novel. Henry II style furniture. Cordoba leather. A few small pictures in huge wooden frames (we can't quite make out whether it's oak or ebony). Chair-rails round the walls.

Enter his valet.

MANDE Monsieur, a Monsieur wishes to see Monsieur.

JACQUES What does he want?

MANDE He's a journalist from the *Gaulois*. He wants to write a column about Monsieur, with Monsieur's collaboration.

JACQUES Show him in!

He comes in. He is:

MORCOL Monsieur. Excuse me if I excuse myself . . .

JACQUES Not at all, not at all. I work for posterity, but I neither disdain nor despise columnists. Take a seat, my dear fellow. Mandé, some port wine for Monsieur.

Morcol takes a seat and drinks his port wine. He smacks his lips and stares at Jacques's partagas.

JACQUES You are a sybarite, my dear fellow.

He offers him a partagas. Morcol bites one end off, lights the other and, as a consequence, starts puffing out smoke.

JACQUES Well, my dear fellow, what good wind brings

you here?

MORCOL The North wind, Maître, the one that will blow the Montgolfier of your fame towards the Mediterranean of your glory! But first of all, may we talk a little about your book. It's true, isn't it, that its hero is one Dicky Ruscombe?

JACQUES Dicky Ruscombe? Not at all. He's called Adalbert de Chamissac-Piéplu.

MORCOL Are you sure he's not called Dicky? . . . a British abbreviation for Richard, according to the dictionary.

JACQUES (hitting himself on the forehead). But of course! I'd forgotten. His second name is Richard, and when he was small his English nanny used to call him Dicky. How could you have guessed that?

MORCOL You admit it, then?

JACQUES (laughing). I admit everything. There is indeed a character called Richard in my next novel. Ah! these journalists!

MORCOL (jumping for joy. Crazy with joy, even). He admits it! He's admitted it!

JACQUES Strange behaviour for a columnist — even a literary one.

MORCOL (calmer). Come on — give him back!

JACQUES What? What's that? Give him back? Give whom back? Upon my life, this man is out of his thinking mind.

MORCOL Come on. We don't want any trouble. Tell me where you're hiding this Richard.

JACQUES But I'm not hiding him! He is very much in evidence. And in any case, if you are interested, and in spite of the fact that your attitude strikes me as being most extraordinary, I can give you his address, because I have given him a house of his own. He lives . . .

MORCOL In the rue Bleue?

JACQUES Because there isn't a rue Mauve in Paris. At number 13A.

MORCOL Is that an odd number?

JACQUES Oh, you know, when it comes to mathematics, I . . .

MORCOL It's of no importance. I shall run all the way!

And, in fact, he goes out running.

JACQUES That's true — is 13A an even number or an odd number? Pah! What do I care. In any case, it's a mauve number.

XI

In the street.

The Doctor gets out of a cab that has stopped at his door. He proffers a moderately satisfactory tip.

THE CABMAN Thanks, gov!

The cab drives off.

THE DOCTOR (ringing). Am I happy? In other words, ought I to get married? Is it very odd to come home to a solitary apartment? Wouldn't it be less odd to know that you were being awaited by a cantankerous termagant like the ones you see in the humorous papers I read? I read them because I provide them for my patients to read in my waiting-room. I even read them very carefully, because I cut out all the caricatures that attack us doctors and, as they say, make a laughing night-scented stock of us. In short, am I happy? In any case, the exercise of my profession affords me a certain satisfaction. Yes, it isn't like the writers whose discussions I overheard just now at my club. Their activities cause them such anguish. Such anxiety! There always seems to be a doubt about their art. And yet it can't be difficult to write a novel, all you have to do is recount a true story. And I certainly know some true stories! But I don't want to become a novelist. I wonder why Hubert, Jean, Jacques and Surget, who honour me with their custom whenever they're suffering from the slightest trifle, never ask me for ideas. But no — they invent them. Ah well (he rings again). They invent them so successfully that they sometimes even lose their characters. It's as if I were to lose my patients!

He laughs. The door opens.

A VOICE IN THE NIGHT Good evening, Doctor.

DOCTOR Well well: good evening, LN. You haven't come to consult me, have you?

LN No, I was on my way home to dress. I'm having supper at the Café Anglais tonight.

DOCTOR A prince? . . .

LN No no; I'm playing hostess.

DOCTOR Lucky man.

He kisses LN on the forehead. Just as he is about to go in, she comes back.

LN Doctor.

DOCTOR What is it, my dear?

LN You know all the writers and journalists in this neighbourhood — you don't by any chance know a M. Lubert, do you?

DOCTOR Indeed I do. He's one of my patients.

LN How is he?

DOCTOR That's a very indiscreet question.

LN Oh, excuse me.

DOCTOR Well well. As a matter of fact — with whom are you having supper this evening?

LN That's a very indiscreet question, Doctor.

DOCTOR Let us say no more, then.

This time he shuts the door behind him.

XII

At no. 13A rue Bleue.

MORCOL Worthy guardian of this building, is M. Chamissac-Piéplu at home?

CONCIERGE No Monsieur.

MORCOL Where might I find him, worthy guardian of this building?

CONCIERGE M. Chamissac-Piéplu is taking supper at the Café Anglais.

MORCOL I shall run all the way!

In the street.

MORCOL (running with his elbows tucked into his sides). And now, en route for the Café Anglais! Every step I take brings me nearer to that centre of filthy lucre, luxury and lordly lewdery where the fortunes of young toffs and handsome old barons are made and lost, where they are dissipated – the fortunes – in the hands of semi-demi-reps and demi-mondaines aux camélias. The place where they eat truffles with foie gras, caviar with lentils, quails *en caisse*, Ostend oysters washed down with Tokay and fire-water, not forgetting the champagne that flows on its noxious and vaporous way from private room to private room. The place where the most famous adulteries are consummated and consumed. The place where Kings debauch midinettes who though chaste nevertheless experience a great need for affection. The place where Russian princes among others come to exhaust their slavonic charm at the same time as their gold roubles.

Zounds! What a good runner I am. I'm not even out of breath.

He arrives at the Café Anglais and is about to go in.

THE PORTER A BIG BURLY MAN Stand back, plebeian! We don't want you sullying our renowned velvets with your sweat.

MORCOL (making a clinking sound with his purse). I'm not short of shekels.

THE PORTER A BIG BURLY MAN What are riches without class?

MORCOL But . . .

THE PORTER A BIG BURLY MAN Stand back, vileyn.

MORCOL All right, all right . . .

He goes off murmuring:
I shall have to resort to cunning.

The Porter a Big Burly Man doesn't hear, owing to a slight case of deafness.

XIII

Still outside the Café Anglais.

A young man and a young lady appear at the door.

THE PORTER A BIG BURLY MAN Halt! young people. Should I let you in?

LN And why, big burly man, should you not let us in?

THE PORTER A BIG BURLY MAN Do you deserve to be let in? I don't know you.

LN You will know me from now on, because I am in full flight. I shall rise high in the hall of fame, and be lauded to the skies. And I am accompanied by a young man of excellent family who is also destined for a brilliant future.

THE PORTER A BIG BURLY MAN I only have your word for it.

LN Come on, let us in, big burly man! Our pockets are full of shekels — and aren't we elegant?

She goes in, followed by Icarus, who smiles timidly at the big burly porter.

THE PORTER A BIG BURLY MAN A very recently -acquired elegance. Still, in our profession, what don't we see, what don't we hear? In our profession you might say that we stand at a window that looks out on to the world. A strange little world — in other words, the world of riot and dissipation. With a hop! and a skip! this riot and dissipation takes place under my very eyes, I know all its mysteries, all its secrets, all its deviations, but one day when I've made my fortune and got my nest-egg tucked away I shall come back here in the guise of a caviarised Russian prince with a beaver coat and astrakhan boots, I'll be as furry as a bear and as abundant as a tip, and I shall experience the joys and fatigues of wild nights which at the moment, seen as a spectacle, rather tend to nauseate me. However that may be, for the moment I shall just watch it go by, this lavish, perfumed life which occasionally jettisons into my outstretched hand the odd complacent half-farthing.

A YOUNG MAN Ho there, burly man, is this the Café Anglais?

THE PORTER A BIG BURLY MAN Yes, milord, it is indeed.

YOUNG MAN In that case, I shall go in.

THE PORTER A BIG BURLY MAN Seeing that you look as if you are weighed down with pounds sterling, our Sesames will open of their own accord.

Which they do (with the aid of a human hand).

The young man goes in.

MAITRE D'HOTEL Has Monsieur reserved his private room?

YOUNG MAN Monsieur Jacques has reserved a table in my name.

MAITRE D'HOTEL Would Monsieur be so good as to remind me of his name?

YOUNG MAN Chamissac-Piéplu.

MAITRE D'HOTEL (bowing) Monsieur . . . This way, please . . .

Chamissac-Piéplu sits down at a table. LN and Icarus are at the next table: a dish of Ostend oysters has just been placed in front of them. There is a sound of little wavelets.

MAITRE D'HOTEL (to Chamissac-Piéplu). Monsieur desires ... Monsieur is waiting for ... Monsieur wishes ... Monsieur requires ...

CHAMISSAC-PIEPLU Couldn't you stop that noise?

MAITRE D'HOTEL What noise, Monsieur?

CHAMISSAC-PIEPLU Can't you hear it?

MAITRE D'HOTEL All I can hear, Monsieur, is joyous, jingling conversations, glasses rhyming with knives and forks and, floating over this ensemble, the sound of the gypsy band pom-pomming the tune that is the latest fashion.

CHAMISSAC-PIEPLU Stupid Maître d'hôtel, I am speaking of the noise those people are making with their Ostend oysters.

MAITRE D'HOTEL Monsieur ... really ... I don't understand.

CHAMISSAC-PIEPLU You don't understand! That's a good one! You don't understand! But you *should* understand, my friend. Come on, get those ostreophagists with their lamellibranches to keep quiet.

MAITRE D'HOTEL Monsieur ... if Monsieur will allow me ...

CHAMISSAC-PIEPLU I will not allow you ...

MAITRE D'HOTEL If Monsieur will allow ... will permit ... me ... I can't hear any noise ... only just the lapping sound of little wavelets which, I would have thought, could hardly inconvenience Monsieur ... but rather, on the contrary, conjure up for him the idea of ozone, health, the open sea ...

CHAMISSAC-PIEPLU That is too much. We shall see.

He gets up and goes over to the next table.

CHAMISSAC-PIEPLU (to Icarus). Monsieur, may I

57

request you to cease making that clatter with your oysters in their shells, it is a noise that I cannot tolerate.

LN (to Icarus). Sock him one.

ICARUS We might perhaps discuss the matter first.

LN There's no way of discussing anything with a lout like that.

ICARUS What do I do, then?

LN You slap his face.

Icarus slaps Chamissac-Piéplu's face.

CHAMMISAC-PIEPLU That was justified, I agree. Here is my card, Monsieur.

ICARUS Thanks. (he puts it in his pocket without reading it).

CHAMISSAC-PIEPLU Well! aren't you going to give me yours?

ICARUS Cards have I none.

CHAMISSAC-PIEPLU You haven't a visiting card? Then I'm not sure that it would be the done thing to fight you.

Enter a gentleman with a long beard.

GENTLEMAN WITH A LONG BEARD Allow me to introduce myself: I am the Marquis de Locrom. I am well versed in affairs of honour. Why beat about the bush? I have some seconds at hand, so you can fight your duel without more ado.

ICARUS I'm not going to interrupt my supper for such a trifle.

CHAMISSAC-PIEPLU And I don't see how . . . in the middle of the night . . .

GENTLEMAN WITH A LONG BEARD You can fight by torch-light. Follow me, Messieurs.

LN Go on, pet. I'll wait for you. You've never fought a duel before, so luck's on your side.

ICARUS All right. If that's the way it is . . .

LN (alone) What a charming young man. I love him, that's quite certain. With one single, unerring bullet he'll kill that gentleman. We live in an age when the duel is just as accepted a custom as it was in the days of the Three Musketeers. No doubt it was the success of that famous novel which for the last generation or two has brought the duel back in fashion. It wasn't practised during the Revolution. Robespierre didn't fight a duel with Danton. Some say, though, that it's officers on the reserve who are responsible for the restoration of this custom. Personally I rather incline to the belief that it's the Three Musketeers. Well anyway, whatever the reason, we women have to resign ourselves to this barbarous practice. For a yea or a nay we run the risk of our Prince Charming coming back to us with a sword-hole or a bullet-hole through him, and sometimes more dead than alive. Icarus! But it's Icarus! I was going to say already, but that wouldn't have been very kind.

ICARUS Yes, here I am. Curious, curious affair.

LN Did you kill him?

ICARUS Far from it. He ran away.

LN The coward.

ICARUS There was a fly waiting outside, the Marquis Thingummy pushes Count what's-his-name into it, and Home, James, and don't spare the horses! Count what's-his-name seemed to be putting up a struggle, perhaps it was more an abduction than a flight.

LN I call that fishily suspicious. Never mind, let's eat our Ostend oysters.

Sound of little wavelets.

59

XIV

HUBERT (sitting in front of a blank piece of paper).
Obviously, I could continue with some of the other
characters, but I'm fond of Icarus and I shan't go on
without him. Ah! Icarus! Icarus! why try to elude the fate
for which I had destined you? Where have you landed, in
attempting to try out your wings? I await your return,
whether voluntary or involuntary. In the meantime, all I
can do is stare, dry-eyed, at that hard, forgotten lake
which, under the hoar-frost, is haunted by the absence of a
character. What a fate — that of a novelist without
characters! Perhaps that is how it will be for all of us, one
day. We won't have any more characters. We shall become
authors in search of characters. The novel will perhaps not
be dead, but it won't have characters in it any more.
Difficult to imagine, a novel without characters. But isn't
all progress, if progress exists, difficult to imagine? To tell
the truth, progress stupefies me. You can now go from
Paris to Nice in less than two days, the Fairy Electricity is
beginning to illuminate the towns and, who knows,
perhaps even the countryside one day, the telegraph
crosses the Atlantic, balloons are soon going to be as
dirigible as horses are driveable: where will progress stop?
Where will it come to rest? In literature the symbolists
have already done away with the arithmetic of metre and
the rigour of rhyme, they'll be abolishing punctuation,
next. Hm! come to think of it, that wouldn't be a bad
idea, a bit of decadent poetry in my novel. In the shape,
for instance, of a professor of . . .

The bell rings.

HUBERT (at the door). Who rings, at this late hour?

A VOICE It's me. Morcol.

HUBERT (opening the door). Have you any news?

He recoils. Morcol enters, preceded by a character in whose back he is holding a pistol.

MORCOL (taking off his beard, and at the same time exclaiming triumphantly): Here he is!

HUBERT Here who is?

MORCOL But — your man!

HUBERT (looking closely at Chamissac-Piéplu). That isn't he.

MORCOL What d'you mean, isn't he! You suspected Jacques of having pinched him from you.

HUBERT I may well have, but my suspicion turns out to have been ill-founded. This gentleman bears absolutely no resemblance to the character who escaped from my papers.
(to Chamissac-Piéplu) Monsieur, I hope you 'will be so good as to excuse Monsieur. There has been a mistake.

Morcol, highly annoyed puts his pistol away.

CHAMISSAC-PIEPLU What sort of a jest is this? I find it distasteful. And you, Monsieur, what have you done with your beard?

MORCOL I put it back in my pocket, to save wear and tear.

CHAMISSAC-PIEPLU And what about my duel?

MORCOL That's none of my business, now.

HUBERT What duel?

MORCOL A pretext. He took it seriously.

CHAMISSAC-PIEPLU Are you implying that my adversary was your accomplice?

MORCOL Involuntarily. As a matter of fact . . . (he falls silent and become wrapt in thought).

HUBERT (to Chamissac-Piéplu). Monsieur, you are free. With our apologies.

CHAMISSAC-PIEPLU It's all very well for you! But my duel is wrecked. I shall pass for a coward. What will people think of me!

MORCOL That's of no interest to us.

CHAMISSAC-PIEPLU I shall go and complain to Monsieur Jacques.

HUBERT Whatever you do, don't do that! An excellent colleague whom I would hate to upset. What can I do, Monsieur, to oblige you, and to right the wrong Monsieur has done you?

CHAMISSAC-PIEPLU I can see only one solution. Take me back to my point of departure and act as my second in this affair of honour.

HUBERT Monsieur, my word is my bond. I am your man.

CHAMISSAC-PIEPLU Come on, then.

HUBERT But where to?

CHAMISSAC-PIEPLU AND MORCOL (ensemble) To the Café Anglais!

XV

At the Café Anglais Icarus and LN are finishing their supper. They are getting outside a bottle of Grand Crémant. LN passes her handbag under the table. Icarus pays the bill and leaves an Icarian tip, that's to say a modest one, because he isn't yet versed in the ways of society. LN tactfully makes it up by slipping an extra louis d'or in the maître d'hôtel's mitt.

MAITRE D'HOTEL Was everything to Monsieur and Madame's liking?

LN Very much to their liking. The Ostend oysters were a bit snotty. The foie gras was a bit bloody. In short, perfect. A de luxe restaurant.

MAITRE D'HOTEL And the duel that was so comfortably despatched in no time at all – that was a pleasure.

ICARUS A mystery, rather.

LN Don't underestimate your merits. You put a vulgarian to flight – it was more than a duel, it was a lesson. Wasn't it, Maître d'hôtel?

MAITRE D'HOTEL Yes, Madame. I hope we shall have the pleasure of seeing you again soon, Madame; and you, Monsieur.

LN and Icarus leave.

MAITRE D'HOTEL What a charming couple – but anyone could predict their future. The young man is no more a nobleman than he is the son of the village notary:

63

he won't go far. She'll find another admirer who will be rich and influential, he'll become jealous, ah, it's the old, old story and I know it by heart. I've read a great many novels and I know what happens next. He'll start making scenes, she'll tell him to go to blazes, he'll react with a noble gesture, he'd rather starve, a confrontation, an impulsive action, and pfft! he's out on his ear. He won't try and find another one because he's still in love with this one and it won't even occur to him that the other one could also provide him with the means of existence. He's not the stuff that pimps are made of. He'll become a drunkard, or a beggar, or maybe he'll even join the Foreign Legion. Well well, here's our erstwhile duellist coming back. Monsieur . . .

CHAMISSAC-PIEPLU Where has the gentleman who was sitting at this table gone?

MAITRE D'HOTEL As Monsieur will be able to observe, he has finished his supper and left with the lady who was accompanying him.

CHAMISSAC-PIEPLU Who was he? Where does he live?

MAITRE D'HOTEL Monsieur, I have no idea; absolutely no idea.

CHAMISSAC-PIEPLU Your ignorance grieves me. My first duel . . . A stain on my honour . . . I think I'm going to cry . . . to miss my first duel . . .

MORCOL Pah! There are as good fish in the sea as ever came out of it.

CHAMISSAC-PIEPLU (suddenly losing his temper). And it's all because of you! Imbecile! Here — here's my card. I'll have at least *one* duel.

MORCOL Monsieur, your request is unacceptable. In my capacity as detective, I don't fight duels; it is my duty, rather, to prevent them.

CHAMISSAC-PIEPLU I can't bear it . . . my poor

duel . . . (he breaks down).

HUBERT Come come, be brave! Look, we'll share a bottle of champagne and then I'll take you back to M. Jacques. But now I come to think of it — perhaps you haven't had supper . . .?

CHAMISSAC-PIEPLU (overwhelmed). I'm hungry.

HUBERT Maître d'hôtel, a table.

MAITRE D'HOTEL This one is awaiting you with open arms.

They sit down at the table that Icarus and LN have vacated.

MAITRE D'HOTEL What would Messieurs like to start with?

CHAMISSAC-PIEPLU Ostend oysters.

XVI

MORCOL Let us sum up the situation and, like the captain of an ocean-going liner, I'll take our bearings. In the first place there is something that I must first of all record: I had a hell of a good meal at the Café Anglais, and for the first time in my life, what's more. Monsieur Lubert is beginning to treat me like a friend, he invites me to sup with him! Perhaps he's forgotten my inferior position, or perhaps I've gone up a peg. Whatever the reason, I had a magnificent meal. The Ostend oyster is a superb animal, the stuffed turkey wasn't bad either, the ptarmigan tart with truffles was remarkable for its delicacy and the little vanilla-flavoured coconut soufflés didn't displease me. In the second place there is a second thing that I must record: the presence at the Café Anglais of the little grisette I saw at the Globe and Two Worlds Tavern with that vague young man who was one metre 77 tall whom I questioned in the approved manner and who isn't Dicky Ruscombe. That they should frequent the Café Anglais was certainly a surprise, but one from which at the moment I see no conclusion to be drawn. In the third place, finally, by manipulating the sextant, the compass and the magnetised needle of my profession — a risky metaphor, for I don't really know if these are in fact the instruments used for this purpose, to take one's bearings, I mean — the only thing left for me to do now is to carry out the routine work of visiting successively all M. Lubert's colleagues, who are numerous, but I am not devoid of patience, nor M. Lubert of the spondulics necessary to support such an enquiry. Finally, in the fourth place, having thus taken our bearings, the only latitude left to me now is to seek the longitude of my hammock, which we shall now do not without pleasure.

XVII

Icarus was up first, he went down to buy some croissants, on credit, which hadn't yet been killed by bad debtors. He went up again, made himself some coffee and breakfasted alone, while LN was still asleep. After which he read his Treatise on Theoretical Mechanics, and the less he understood it the more he enjoyed it.

After that LN woke up, and all was Laughter and Frolic; then she started her day not with croissants and coffee, but with brawn salad, to which she was very partial, and a few good glasses of red wine, a drink which she particularly appreciated.

She worked in the afternoons and earned a great deal of money, thus amplifying a nest-egg which in the near future would enable her to change her profession. Icarus pottered about in the modest apartment and, after taking great pains over his toilet, later in the day went down to drink some absinthes at the Globe and Two Worlds Tavern while he waited for LN to reappear. Then they went and had supper, but since the strange episode of the abortive duel they avoided the Café Anglais; in any case LN considered that it was after all a bit expensive.

Sometimes LN was busy in the evenings too, but this didn't particularly surprise Icarus.

XVIII

Hubert is smoking a partagas sitting in front of some blank sheets of paper. He is melancholically drinking port wine. The bell rings. It's Morcol.

MORCOL Monsieur, I have come to give you an account of my mission.

HUBERT (wearily). Still negative, your account?

MORCOL (enthusiastically). Still negative. But it's the details that count.

HUBERT (very wearily). I'm listening.

MORCOL (delighted) Monsieur, I don't know how to express my gratitude in so far as the mission you have entrusted to me is concerned. I have never yet performed such an interesting mission. Yes, Monsieur, now I know all your colleagues personally! There is not a single novelist whom I have not auscultated, be he a worldling, a naturalist, a symbolist, a regionalist, an historian, or no matter what. I have even included epic poets in my enquiry: they are a rare breed, it is true, but we mustn't neglect any possibility. And you cannot but admire, Monsieur, my intelligence and initiative: I have even visited our playwrights.

HUBERT That was pretty useless.

MORCOL I don't see why. There are characters in plays, as well. In fact, that's all there is.

HUBERT Yes, but they aren't the same. A character in a novel can't become a character in a play.

MORCOL I beg your pardon, I beg your pardon, Monsieur Lubert. I don't agree. I don't see why a character in a novel can't become a character in a play. And to support my argument, let me cite certain plays that have been adapted from novels. For example, M. de Goncourt and his Fille Elisa, it was a novel, and then it became a play, and yet they are the same characters. And a character in a novel may even turn into a singer. Manon, for example, which was a novel and then became an opera (and perhaps even a comic opera). I don't see what you can find to say to that. Ha ha! I'm beginning to understand a bit about these things now. I've rubbed up against so many members of your corporation that it's made me quite phosphorescent.

HUBERT I beg your pardon! I beg your pardon! they are not the *same* characters, they are different ones. They bear the same name, but they have *nothing* in common, d'you hear? — NOTHING. Is the third rate actress whining Adieu, our little table — the same as the Abbé Prévost's Manon Lescaut? No, mister detective. No: they are two different characters.

MORCOL Don't agree.

HUBERT (nauseated). In any case, even if you are now showing signs of literary pretentions, you haven't had much success in the field of detection.

MORCOL Patience! patience! your Dicky won't elude me for long.

HUBERT My Dicky? Why do you call him Dicky?

MORCOL I call him Dicky because you call him Dicky.

HUBERT I don't call him Dicky, I call him Icarus.

MORCOL First I've heard of it. Didn't you say: I shan't be able to work until the mystery's solved and Dicky Ruscombe's back? Ruscombe was his surname, I presumed.

HUBERT His name is Icarus, and that's that.

MORCOL And here have I been looking everywhere for a Dicky . . . What did you say it was, then: Icarus? Just one word?

HUBERT Yes. I see eh are you ess.

MORCOL Icarus? That's not a Christian name, I've never seen it in the calendar of saints. It's his surname, is it?

HUBERT It's just a name, that's all.

MORCOL Then I'll have to start my enquiry again from scratch, I suppose?

HUBERT Obviously, if you were looking for a Dicky.

MORCOL Well well, that's a mistake that's going to cost you dear, Monsieur Lubert. I'll need a further advance of twenty louis.

HUBERT You are dangerously ruining me. And how can I tell that you'll know better how to set about it from now on?

MORCOL Monsieur, with the elements that I have hitherto neglected, the plot now thickens around the name of Icarus. But as in the case of a mayonnaise, this can only be a good sign, and I am confident that what is now about to happen in the Stendhalian phenomenon of crystallisation. It is now no more than a question of a centimetre.

XIX

At the Globe and Two Worlds Tavern.

ICARUS (sitting in front of his fifth absinthe). I might compare absinthe to a Montgolfier. It elevates the spirit as the balloon elevates the nacelle. It transports the soul as the balloon transports the traveller. It multiplies the mirages of the imagination as the balloon multiplies one's points of view over the terrestial sphere. It is the flux which carries dreams as the balloon allows itself to be guided by the wind. Let us drink, then, let us swim in the milky, greenish wave of disseminated oneiric images, in the company of my surrounding habitués: their faces are sinister but their absinthed hearts absent themselves along abstruse and maybe abyssine abscissae.

LN (coming in) My pet! that's your howmanieth?

ICARUS My seventh.

LN But you've only got five saucers.

ICARUS I was anticipating. I'm an anticipatory character.

LN You're in a good mood, I see. Waiter, the same. Weren't you bored without me?

ICARUS Not at all. I was waiting for you.

LN Would you have been equally pleased to wait longer for me?

ICARUS I'll wait for you as long as you tell me to.

LN Several days. More than a week, maybe.

ICARUS Am I allowed to ask why?

LN I'm going to change my job. My profession. I made the decision all by myself in my little head because of my love for you. The profession I've been following, one of the oldest in the world, as the saying goes . . .

ICARUS Am I allowed to know what it is?

LN Don't let's talk about it any more, since I'm changing it. I'm going to become a modiste or a dressmaker or something like that. I'm going to the provinces to collect an inheritance and when I come back I shall set myself up in business. I'll leave you some money to live on while I'm away, you must take good care of it, you must use it reasonably, you mustn't go to the Café Anglais, for instance and, in general, be careful! Be very careful! Be on your guard! Never stop being on your guard!

ICARUS We'll do our best.

LN I'm rather worried about leaving you on your own.

ICARUS I shall think of you all the time, and I'll be on my guard against everyone.

LN Then, waiter! — another absinthe.

XX

MORCOL (enters and sits down at a table. To the waiter). Waiter, a beer.

(to Morcol). There they are. They're both sitting over there. The girl doesn't interest me because I haven't got to reclaim her. Waiter!

WAITER Yes, Monsieur. Was the beer tepid?

MORCOL No, no. Excellent, your beer. That wasn't why I called you.

WAITER That's what I thought.

MORCOL That young man over there with that young lady, the third table from the right in the back row, you don't by any chance know his name, do you?

WAITER Let's have a look. The third table from the right in the back row? From my right or from their right?

MORCOL From my right. Hurry up, they're just paying.

WAITER Ah, you mean the young man who's just paying? Don't you believe it, Monsieur, he isn't paying. It's an illusion. He only looks as if he is. It's actually the young lady who's paying: just one of those things.

MORCOL But the name! Quick! They're leaving.

WAITER The name? The name of the young person?

MORCOL No! The name of the young man, dark brown hair et caetera.

LN (outside). Did you see that fellow? It's you he's looking for. Don't ever set foot in here again.

ICARUS Don't worry. Without you I shall lose my taste for absinthe.

MORCOL (outside). He may be the one. He's disappeared. Meanwhile, I'm tightening my net. Don't let's be in too much of a hurry, though, and don't let's neglect our other work. After all, this isn't the only thing I have to do.

XXI

Mme DE CHAMPVAUX It's quite obvious – you don't love me any more.

HUBERT Oh come, of course I do.

Mme DE CHAMPVAUX Well then ... your lack of ardour ... for the last few weeks ... explain that ...

HUBERT You have to have all your i's dotted. I have some worries, with a dot on the i.

Mme DE CHAMPVAUX What worries, if you please?

HUBERT They're ... professional worries ...

Mme DE CHAMPVAUX I don't see how anyone can have worries in your profession.

HUBERT We have them just as much as people do in any other profession. More, even.

Mme DE CHAMPVAUX You make me laugh. You sit down at your table in your slippers, you pick up a pen and you write whatever comes into your head without putting yourself out too much, afterwards you even find someone to publish you and give you some money. Writers live like fighting cocks. Worries – you make me laugh.

HUBERT Let us draw a veil over your singular ideas, on which I shall refrain from commenting. I assure you that I have some serious anxieties, but I don't want to bore you with them.

Mme DE CHAMPVAUX Let's see. What anxieties?

HUBERT It's difficult to explain.

Mme DE CHAMPVAUX I suppose you think I'm stupid?

HUBERT Far from it, far from it, but you will find it difficult to believe me.

Mme DE CHAMPVAUX That's just what I thought; I can smell a bad excuse hiding somewhere.

HUBERT Not bad: excellent, legitimate.

Mme DE CHAMPVAUX I still don't know what it is.

HUBERT Do you want me to tell you?

Mme DE CHAMPVAUX Your lack of ardour would offend me if it isn't based on serious worries . . .

HUBERT Well, it's like this. I'd just started a novel . . .

Mme DE CHAMPVAUX That isn't a worry for you, and it doesn't bore me. It might bore the people who have to read it, of course.

HUBERT (shrugs his shoulders and continues). I'd written some ten or fifteen pages when my chief character, Icarus, disappeared. Impossible to continue!

Mme DE CHAMPVAUX And all you can do about it is be sorry for yourself?

HUBERT Not at all. I've taken action. I've engaged a detective, a specialist in Subtle Shadowing, to track him down.

Mme DE CHAMPVAUX And what is the name of this individual?

HUBERT Morcol.

Mme DE CHAMPVAUX Pah! Morcol? He's absolutely useless! I know him very well. My husband has engaged him to follow me. Don't worry, he doesn't know I'm here. I read the reports he sends to Julien. They're laughable.

HUBERT At least he takes some trouble.

Mme DE CHAMPVAUX And why don't you look for your Icarus yourself?

HUBERT What would be the use of detectives?

Mme DE CHAMPVAUX Morcol will never find him for you. He's hopeless — I'm your proof of that.

HUBERT I believe in him: I'm waiting.

Mme DE CHAMPVAUX You could carry on without this Icarus.

HUBERT Impossible.

Mme DE CHAMPVAUX Why not make the best of it — write something else and get back your ardour.

HUBERT Oh! you get on my nerves! Mind your own business and stop telling me what to do. You don't know the slightest thing about my work, not the slightest, slightest thing. You understand?

Mme DE CHAMPVAUX Yes, Hubert. I'll come back when you've started work again.

HUBERT That's right, that's right.
She lowers her veil and leaves.
In the street, Morcol follows her.

XXII

DOCTOR Come in, my dear fellow. I hope there's nothing seriously wrong with you. Though that's an insipid question, because it's *I* who should tell *you*. But first of all, who was that freak of nature you sent me the other day?

HUBERT That's just it. He has an immediate relevance to my personal troubles.

DOCTOR I'm listening.

HUBERT Doctor, I'm blushing, but it's a particularly intimate question that brings me here.

DOCTOR Well, blushing is virtue's colour, as the saying goes, but you needn't bother to blush when you're talking to your doctor.

HUBERT The thing... you see... well, the thing is, I'm lacking in, er, ardour...

DOCTOR Simple as Simon Pure! Take an aphrodisiac.

HUBERT Wouldn't do any good. It's my morale.

DOCTOR If you know better than I what the matter is with you, why come and consult me?

HUBERT It has something to do with my trade.

DOCTOR You haven't a trade, you have a profession.

HUBERT Trade or profession or nothing at all, at all events, I write; and I write novels. And the hero of my next novel has flown.

DOCTOR I know; your freak told me.

HUBERT That freak is a detective.

DOCTOR A madman. He suspected *me*!

HUBERT You must excuse him.

DOCTOR And why has your hero flown? Did he have anything to complain about?

HUBERT What should he have to complain about? He'd only existed for a few pages.

DOCTOR Perhaps you were preparing a bitter fate for him.

HUBERT Not in my opinion.

DOCTOR Perhaps in his.

HUBERT Doctor, I came to consult you about myself, not about Icarus.

DOCTOR He's called Icarus now, is he?

HUBERT He's always been called that.

DOCTOR Ah! In any case, it's a difficult name to bear.

HUBERT You're more worried about him than you are about me! But *I'm* the one with the problem. Until he's found.

DOCTOR Well — you must just be patient.

HUBERT Patient!

DOCTOR A sedative, then. Some orange-blossom water. Some herb tea. That can't do you any harm.

HUBERT You were recommending an aphrodisiac not long ago, and now it's a sedative: I want neither the one nor the other.

DOCTOR That's the modern patient all over. They'd like to dictate our prescriptions to us!

HUBERT None of this gives me back my Icarus.

DOCTOR I'm not a detective.

HUBERT And then, I'm becoming irritable. Very irritable. Can't you really do anything for me?

DOCTOR Take some bicarbonate of soda . . . it's a miracle remedy . . .

HUBERT I don't believe in it.

DOCTOR There's a new pharmacofugal method I can try on you.

HUBERT Thanks! I haven't got to that point yet.

DOCTOR Well then, I'll write you out a classic prescription: herb tea on rising, and a little orange-blossom water on retiring. That'll be two francs.

HUBERT Thank you, Doctor, but I'm in a very bad mood.

DOCTOR What do you expect — that's life.

XXIII

JEAN Well, my dear Jacques, how far have you got with your novel?

JACQUES My Chamissac-Piéplu nearly fought a duel, but I'm keeping that episode for later on. After the adultery that has just taken place. In a fly.

JEAN I can't help observing, my dear Jacques: adultery in a fly — what could be more banal?

JACQUES Yes, but my fly is mauve.

JEAN There's no such thing.

JACQUES That's the way I see it.

JEAN Perhaps you have an impressionistic eye?

SURGET (insurgent). My friends, I've just finished a novel which is going to sell like hot cakes.

JEAN What's it about?

SURGET Adultery. And in a fly, what's more.

JACQUES (anxiously) I hope it isn't mauve?

SURGET What an extraordinary idea. No. It's . . . black. Actually, I've never thought about the colour of flies. They're black, I think. In any case, seeing what takes place in them . . .

JEAN Well, *my* adultery takes place in a bed.

SURGET You're indecent.

JEAN No, only daring. And I'd be even more so if the

laws were not so strict. By the way, my friends, haven't you a feeling that you're under constant surveillance?

JACQUES Yes indeed! In a most offensive fashion.

SURGET Alas! The responsibility is mine. Lubert has lost one of his characters, and I advised him to call in the famous Morcol. Who suspects us all. Why, only the other day I was helping a children's nurse to cross the boulevard with her perambulator . . . an heroic act, in view of the infernal traffic. Flies and private carriages were irrupting from all sides. Well, the children's nurse — was he!

JACQUES I know exactly what you mean! I was thinking of installing running water in my flat. A plumber called, and flooded the whole place. The plumber — was he!

JEAN The other day, in a restaurant, a clumsy waiter spilt the haricot mutton over my waistcoat. The haricot mutton — was he! That is . . . I mean . . .

JACQUES Ah! — here *is* Lubert.

HUBERT Messieurs . . .

JEAN My dear Lubert, we were just talking about you.

JACQUES Yes, we were saying that your detective was beginning to inconvenience us rather too much.

HUBERT What detective . . .

SURGET You know very well.

HUBERT Traitor! Is that the way you keep a secret?

SURGET One simply can't work in peace any more.

JACQUES We consider this espionage offensive.

JEAN Not to say disturbing and boring.

SURGET All the more so as I'd given you my word of honour.

JACQUES And we could have given you ours, too.

JEAN Most certainly.

SURGET So please tell your detective . . .

JACQUES . . . to stop . . .

JEAN . . . meddling . . .

HUBERT Messieurs . . . your attack on me amounts to veritable aggression . . . I can see only one answer . . .

THE THREE OTHERS A duel? Agreed!

HUBERT Messieurs, my seconds will call on each and every one of you. I shall rapierise you all! Adieu!

Exit.

SURGET He really *is* in a bad mood.

JACQUES How very convenient. I wanted to have a duel in my novel. I shall be able to take notes and modify the reality of the description.

JEAN Aren't you modern!

XXIV

The pallid dawn was shrouding with its pearl-grey mantles the trees in the Bois de Boulogne and their dew. Five flies approaching from the four quarters of the horizon caused sinister reverberations in the cobblestones, in the asphalt, and even in the plain mud. In these flies were seated black-garbed men as grave an antipyrine sachets and, when the above-mentioned flies came to a halt, the men in black got out of them. They were seventeen in number: four duellists, eight seconds, one doctor and four journalists. Now they are tossing a coin, even though they have no money to lose, nor time to waste. The reason they are doing this is to decide on the first duel. For if there are four duellists, there are to be three duels, and not two as might legitimately be supposed. One of these gentlemen is in fact to fight the three others in succession. This has never been known since Richelieu's day, which explains the presence of the journalists. Hubert is to fight Jean first. A pale sunbeam attempts to pierce the clouds; it doesn't succeed. Hubert, the more skilful, scratches Jean, who considers that this hurts, but doesn't say too much about it. They go on to the second duel, Jacques is at the receiving end of a lunge, a fine thrust in the stomach, the doctor hastily sews him up, hoping there's better to come. They ask Hubert if he's tired. Not at all. The journalists take due note of this fact. It's Surget's turn to come and cross swords now, but his adversary is made of steel, and Surget bites the grass because he finds the thrust he's just received so painful. He is carried off, too. The journalists make their way back to their gazettes. Hubert goes home. The sun finally manages to rapierise the clouds that were obnubilating it. The adversaries have not been reconciled.

XXV

LN's prolonged absence was worrying Icarus. So he went back to absinthe, but not to the Globe and Two Worlds Tavern. He chose others, and a different one each day. He also read the gazettes there, even though for the most part their stories remained a mystery to him.

At the Three Storks Tavern he asks for *Le Gaulois*, which is brought to him attached in a bit of wood, as if it were a flag.

He waves it, and then on the front page reads FOUR LITERARY MUSKETEERS FIGHT A DUEL OVER A QUESTION OF TECHNIQUE. That was the headline. There were no details about the aforesaid question of technique, and this intrigued Icarus to the highest degree; on the other hand he was no little proud to learn that his originator had so successfully crossed swords with the three others.

ICARUS (full of enthusiasm) What a man! What a blade!

Even so, he is surprised not to find anything about himself. Not a word about Icarus. Some talk about technique, but all very vague. These gentlemen are quarrelling over a technical question, right, but what question, that remains vague, that remains very vague.

ICARUS (to Icarus) I'm a little disappointed.

Disappointed not to see his name in the paper? Already? And yet he doesn't feel any particular reverence for the gazettes. This is a feeling that worms its way into you stealthily and surreptitiously; you cast a vague, a very vague, eye over the gazettes, and then one fine day there you are wanting to see your name in them, wanting to see your name in print. Temptation.

Well, no: it isn't that — that isn't what makes Icarus say: I'm disappointed. He's disappointed because Hubert hasn't mentioned him. What! Could he have forgotten him? Already! It's obvious that he, Icarus, is the cause of the triel, but Hubert might have said so.

Perhaps it's a trick. Perhaps he (Hubert) doesn't want him (Icarus) to know that he (Hubert) is trying to find him (Icarus). Perhaps it was even that fellow the other day who advised him not to. Certainly. And the technical question — is himself.

And so, says Icarus to himself, behind the technical question there is a living character: himself. The technical question is a mask, a decoy, to dupe the public and the journalists, and to deceive him (Icarus). But Icarus is not deceived.

Icarus suddenly feels like seeing the venue of the triel, in other words the Bois de Boulogne, in short, to commit an imprudent act. Instead of studying the mechanics of solid bodies, here he is making his way towards the West, according to the sun, which might well have led him to Levallois-Perret, but fortunately he sees a policeman and asks him the way. You'd better take an omnibus, the constable advises him. Icarus prefers to walk. It'll take you a good hour, says the constable.

ICARUS That doesn't matter. Please tell me the way.

CONSTABLE A laborious and complicated undertaking. Just keep going in that direction (gesture). One thing leading to another, you'll get there in the end.

Icarus is walking through the streets, beset by constant dangers. Carriages, coachmen and horses seem to have entered into a conspiracy to run him over, not to mention hand-carts, men carrying planks and ladders, divers waggons et caetera et caetera. He is always having to stand aside to the right, to stand aside to the left, constant danger (as we have already said). Men are painting, men are washing down façades — more dangers. Icarus keeps going and makes light of all these perils. Paris becomes an infernal city, the noise of the omnibus wheels on the cobblestones reverberates in the ears like the trumpets of a penultimate Judgment. And the cries of the people, the cries of newspaper sellers, of glaziers, of scavengers, of florists, of beggars, of this one and that one, oh la la, what a racket.

Which subsides a little when you get to the Place de L'Etoile. Another (and different) constable shows Icarus the way to the Porte Maillot. Icarus sits down on a bench in the Avenue de la Grande-Armée and all of a sudden, what does he see going by? a horseless carriage in which are seated two bears. It is moving, this carriage, it is even moving quite fast, back-firing and odoriferous, and the horses rear as it passes, and the pedestrians either admire it or fall into a panic.

ICARUS Well, I haven't wasted my time today, now I've seen that.

He starts on his way again, he also sees men in caps moving their shanks up and down while sitting astride a frame supported by two wheels; they too are moving, they're even moving quite fast, sometimes faster than the horseless carriages, for there are several of them in this district and, what's more, there are traders in these machines all along this Avenue de la Grande-Armée. All of which interests Icarus extremely.

An automobile carriage is standing in a shed, a man is messing about with its innards. This shed is a garage; this man is a mechanic.

Icarus goes up to him.

ICARUS Excuse me, Monsieur: may I speak to you?

MECHANIC You already have.

ICARUS What you have there is indeed, is it not, a carriage that moves without horses?

87

MECHANIC Ay. That carriage moves without horses, and that's why it's called an automobile carriage.

ICARUS And what makes it move?

MECHANIC The Fairy Electricity.

ICARUS Please be so good as to give me further details.

MECHANIC Young man, you are right to take an interest in this, for This is the future. We shall soon be able to drive at 25 miles an hour, a speed which it will be difficult to exceed. We shall be able to go to Le Havre in five hours, to Marseilles in a day. I can imagine, in the future, there being terminals along the roads at which people will be able to recharge their accumulators. For I am in favour of Electricity and Progress. Don't talk to me about petroleum. Just look at that.

A carriage passes, emitting a great deal of noise and stinking gases.

MECHANIC No, don't talk to me about petroleum, it makes a vile noise, it stinks, it explodes — no customer will ever put up with that. And then, if the number of automobile carriages were to increase, there wouldn't be enough petroleum in the world, you can take it from me.

ICARUS All this seems worthy of attention.

MECHANIC No, believe me, the electric carriage is the future. Would you like to come for a ride with me? I've repaired that contrary little thing, that little contraption, and now things are going to hum. You'll see how stunning it is.

Icarus gets in, the carriage does more than 22 m.p.h.

ICARUS It feels as if we were going to take wing!

MECHANIC Young man, if you're so interested, come and work in this branch of industry — you could earn some money.

ICARUS Thank you for your advice, Monsieur.

MECHANIC Unless you'd like to *buy* an automobile, of course.

ICARUS I don't think I have the means.

MECHANIC Buy yourself a Velocipede, then. Hang it — be modern!

ICARUS I'll think about it, Monsieur. I'll think about it. Many thanks.

He disappears in the direction of the Bois de Boulogne.

ICARUS That technical question torments me. Was it a genuine technical question, or was it really the question of my existence? By a genuine technical question I mean, for example, the division of a novel into books and chapters, the placing of descriptions, the choice of first names and patronymics, the use of dashes or inverted commas to indicate dialogue, or small caps for the names of the protagonists as in printed plays or the works of the Countess de Ségur. Goodness, that's a bird singing.

XXVI

DOCTOR Well, my friend, how is our poor atrophied health?

SURGET I'm doing my best.

DOCTOR Let's have a little look at that wound (he looks). Pah — just a trifle. I'll take out the surgical stitches, and your scar will be magnificent. Bring me my scissors.

His scissors are brought and he cuts out the surgical stitches.

DOCTOR And now you can go back to your work.

SURGET In other words: send my novel to certain selected critics.

DOCTOR That's something our poor friend Hubert isn't in a position to do.

SURGET Poor friend, indeed! You're forgetting that he ripped me open.

DOCTOR Yes, but you're publishing your novel, and he can't publish his. Just think! What if it had happened to you, eh? — what if one of your characters were to disappear . . .

SURGET Doctor, as the saying goes: ne ultra crepidam! This is no longer medicine!

DOCTOR Oh yes it is: it's mental medicine, and nothing is foreign to mental medicine.

SURGET Then perhaps I'm mad: I've just started a new novel, and I am inordinately pleased with my hero.

DOCTOR Don't make him the flighty type.

SURGET I'll take care not to.

XXVII

DOCTOR Well, is our stomach healing?

JACQUES Marvellously. Look.

DOCTOR A lovely scar. You're as good as new.

JACQUES Can't you see anything special about my scar?

DOCTOR Luckily for you — not a thing.

JACQUES Wouldn't you say it was rather mauve?

DOCTOR Mauve, mauve. So it is. It *is* somewhat as you describe it . . . somewhat mauve. What a sensitive appreciation of colours you have! You have a painter's eye!

JACQUES The eye of the descriptive prose-writer. I'm the descriptive type. Description for description's sake. If I had to, I could do without characters.

DOCTOR You aren't like our poor friend Hubert.

JACQUES Poor friend indeed! That clumsy swashbuckler who accidently ripped me open.

DOCTOR Just think if it had happened to you, a character running away.

JACQUES I shouldn't have minded. There's only one thing that matters to me: the colour mauve.

XXVIII

DOCTOR Well, how's our scratch?

JEAN Scratch indeed! Funny, aren't you. It still hurts.

DOCTOR Compared with Jacques and Surget, you've no cause for complaint.

JEAN Always the optimist.

DOCTOR And if, like our poor friend Hubert . . .

JEAN Hubert! He bores us to death with his Icarus. The idea! — suspecting us! Hiring a detective to follow us! Challenging us to a duel! In which we get wounded, what's more. There's no justice!

DOCTOR None of this is so very terrible when you compare it with losing a character. Just think — what if that had happened to you?

JEAN There are as good characters in the pool as ever came out of it! In any case, I have a file full of characters, hundreds of them, on the strength of which I can go on producing works based entirely on adultery and on ultra modern fin-de-siècle sentiments which may well soon be out of date, but which at the moment are extremely lucrative.

DOCTOR What are you complaining about, then?

JEAN My physical scratch.

XXIX

Icarus went to the Avenue de la Grande-Armée every day, now. Having first become a connoisseur of cycles, and then of electric or petroliphagous automobile carriages, when he conversed with the mechanics there it was with a certain competence — an illusory competence but one which had nevertheless resulted, even, in an offer of work. For the moment he had nothing to worry about from the material point of view, so he refused without actually saying no. He would occasionally take advantage of the offer of a ride from a well-intentioned or boastful garage-proprietor, and they would go two or three hundred yards in the chuff-chuff. There were even times when Icarus took the wheel.

At other times he went to the Bois de Boulogne. He lay down on the grass, listened to the little birds singing and watched the elegant carriages passing by.

One day, when he was walking quietly along an avenue, a horse suddenly bolted. He jumped for its head and stopped it.

Mme DE CHAMPVAUX Oh! what a handsome young man! Such courage! How exciting! Monsieur — come and sit beside me, I'll drive you to a chemist's and we'll get him to put some arnica on your bruises.

ICARUS Thank you, Madame, I'd like some arnica.

At the chemist's.

Mme DE CHAMPVAUX Well, young man, are you feeling better now?

ICARUS Yes, Madame.

CHEMIST That'll be fifty centimes.

ICARUS That's expensive.

Mme DE CHAMPVAUX And what's more, he's poor! Handsome and poor! Here, chemist, here are your fifty centimes.

They go out.

Mme DE CHAMPVAUX What do you do in life, young man?

ICARUS Nothing, Madame.

Mme DE CHAMPVAUX Idle! Handsome, poor and idle! As in a fashionable novel! A Bohemian, if I understand aright. What a marvellous day!

Mme de Champvaux climbs back into her landau.

Mme DE CHAMPVAUX And we must part so soon! But I hope we shall see each other again.

ICARUS Yes, Madame.

Mme DE CHAMPVAUX Where do you live?

ICARUS I have no fixed address.

Mme DE CHAMPVAUX He's wonderful.

ICARUS Madame, don't let's exaggerate.

Mme DE CHAMPVAUX And . . . your name?

ICARUS Icarus, Madame.

Mme DE CHAMPVAUX And he's called Icarus! (dumbfounded). Icarus? Really Icarus? (pulling herself together). And my name, Monsieur, is Madame de Prébeuf.

ICARUS How do you do, Madame.

Mme DE CHAMPVAUX Would you allow me to thank you for your heroic act by inviting you to come and take a finger of port wine with me? My husband will pour it for you himself.

ICARUS It's tempting, naturally.

Mme DE CHAMPVAUX Tomorrow! I insist. Where can my coachman call for you?

ICARUS Er . . . um . . .

Mme DE CHAMPVAUX You certainly won't refuse a little finger of port wine. Where, then?

ICARUS Well, er . . . at the Globe and Two Worlds Tavern at absinthe time . . .

Mme DE CHAMPVAUX Handsomely spoken, handsome Icarus. My landau will be there.

She departs: so does her landau.

ICARUS Perhaps I ought to be more on my guard.

XXX

At the doctor's.

DOCTOR Well, my dear friend?

HUBERT I'm much better.

DOCTOR My little remedy?

HUBERT Not at all! No — my triel, first, and then Morcol. The former got rid of my bad mood, and the latter is on Icarus's track and has practically found him. As soon as I get him back I can go on with my novel.

DOCTOR He may have changed.

HUBERT Why should he have changed? You're trying to demoralise me, doctor.

DOCTOR We have to see life as it is. Yes, supposing he's changed! You must have confidence in yourself, but not too much in him. And to have confidence in yourself, you must go on drinking the herb tea.

HUBERT You make me feel terrible!

DOCTOR You mustn't count your chickens . . .

HUBERT You're making me see everything in a blacker and blacker light.

DOCTOR Herb tea! Herb tea! that's the only remedy, apart from bicarbonate and my new method.

HUBERT You still haven't quite deprived me of all hope.

DOCTOR You're beyond treatment.

Hubert goes home and drinks a cup of herb tea all the same. He absent-mindedly turns over the blank pages of his next novel.

HUBERT When Icarus comes back I shall orient him in the direction of decadent poetry, so that he really belongs to his time, and I shall give him a professor of irregular prosody and free-versery, M. Maîtretout, whom I've invented these last few days. M. Maîtretout, has a daughter Adelaide, a real pearl, with fairy fingers. She falls, that's certain, in love with the pupil. I can see a marriage looming on the horizon. This pure person will serve as a counterbalance to the fin-de-siècle characteristics with which I intend to imbue Icarus. And in any case, I shan't have long to wait until all this happens. Morcol has promised to bring him back within the next twenty-four hours. I don't think he's spoofing. He did make a mistake once but once is by no means always, and I think he's conscientious. Obviously Icarus will have seen the great wide world during his flight and he may well have changed, as Dr. Lajoie said. In which case we'll think again. In the meantime, let's live on hope and herb tea.

XXXI

The Globe and Two Worlds Tavern. Enter Icarus.

WAITER A ghost!

ICARUS An absinthe!

WAITER And how is Mademoiselle LN?

ICARUS LU-sive.

WAITER Ah, Monsieur Icarus, we've missed you, and I'll bring you your drink with all celerity.

He actually does so.
Icarus studies a gazette.

WAITER Monsieur Icarus, pardon me for disturbing you in your insipid reading, but there's a coachman waiting for you. He says you know all about it.

ICARUS I do. I'm off, then!

He pays, stands up and goes out.

COACHMAN (in a falsetto voice) Get in, my prince. A lady awaits you.

ICARUS I know.

He gets in.

COACHMAN Giddy-up, Cocotte! (to the coachman). We've got him.

ICARUS So I'm on my way to see a society lady and drink a finger of port wine. On second thoughts, it's extremely risky. I was living in concealment and I allowed myself to be persuaded to leave my retreat. And in any case, I don't love the lady, it isn't out of love that I'm going to see her, that wouldn't be fair to LN, I'm going out of pure curiosity, I think I'm definitely making a mistake, a big mistake.

Coachman, stop!

(The coachman accelerates).

Yes but, he isn't slowing down. Coachman, stop!

(The coachman keeps on accelerating, the horse strikes sparks with all four shoes). What a devilish pace! I couldn't even jump out at this speed! And anyway, where's he going? What district is he making for? But what do I see? Isn't this the street M. Lubert lives in? And there's his house, and there's his door. Drive on, coachman! Drive on! The beast, he isn't, he's stopping.

Icarus jumps down on the pavement and takes wing. Morcol, who had been hanging on behind the fly, jumps off at the same time as Icarus and grabs hold of him. The coachman, who has climbed down from his seat, gives him a helping hand. When he sees that the coachman is none other than Mme de Champvaux, Icarus gives up all resistance.

ICARUS (dejected). What an innocent I was, I never knew that a woman could be such a traitress!

Mme DE CHAMPVAUX And he insults me, the scoundrel!

MORCOL Come on, Monsieur, come on up. M. Lubert's waiting for you.

Icarus hangs his head, a sign of resignation.

MORCOL (to Mme de Champvaux) Thank you, Madame. M. de Champvaux will never know of his misfortune.

Mme DE CHAMPVAUX Monsieur, you are a gentleman.

MORCOL Let's go up and put Icarus back between M. Lubert's pages.

99

XXXII

At the Club.

JEAN My dear fellow, everything is going very well for me. How about you?

JACQUES No less well. Thanks to the duel, I've been able to perfect that of Chamissac-Piéplu. As I'd given you to understand, the experience enabled me to describe it in a way that has nothing in common with reality.

JEAN Won't the reader be put off by the lack of verisimilitude?

JACQUES It's possible. What's that to me? I shall be read in half a century's time. By posterity.

JEAN Hm! Do you think people will still be interested in adultery and duels then? Times change.

JACQUES Not to that point.

JEAN Personally, as I'm incapable of foreseeing the future I'm quite happy with my contemporaries. I know them, and I hope they will recognise me.

SURGET (insurgent) My friends! How are you?

JEAN Extremely well — and you?

SURGET In great fettle. Doctor Lajoie is unique.

JEAN Because of that triel the gazettes are always mentioning our names, but you benefit from it more particularly, as your novel has just come out.

SURGET I'm not complaining. The bookshops are

simply shovelling them out, and my publisher wants me to get a new one under way.

JEAN Which you have done, no doubt.

SURGET Exactly. And it will be dynamite, to coin an expression.

JACQUES May one know?

SURGET In my next work, the peaceable Corentin Durendal will perpetrate an abominable crime.

HUBERT Messieurs!

THE OTHERS Monsieur.

HUBERT Let's make it up, shall we? I did rapierise you, but I admit that my suspicions of you were unjustified. My Icarus has been found.

THE OTHERS Really?

HUBERT Yes indeed! My detective brought him back to me, bound hand and foot, and I started work again immediately. Let's make it up, shall we?

THE OTHERS Consider it done! We are reconciled.

HUBERT Champagne!

They drink a bottle of champagne, which makes a gritty sound under their teeth.

XXXIII

Hubert was working; in his study, decorated with Cordoba leather and dusky velvets, protective chair-rails, elaborate wainscotting and pictures with wide frames, though they were sometimes only miniatures, he was aligning lines upon lines which were causing Icarus's fate to proceed in directions known only to himself. Icarus was supposed never to have met either LN or Mme de Champvaux and he seemed to have forgotten the knowledge he had never had either of statics or kinematics. He had, on the other hand, had several innocent conversations with Adelaide, the daughter of his professor of symbolist rhetoric, M. Maîtretout. Much against his will, however. Hubert couldn't stop him thinking about LN, but each time this happened he made a big blot on the paper.

The housekeeper-cook announced that luncheon was served. She was called Eurtrude, a rare but not exceptional Christian name. Hubert carefully put away the pages he had written in a morocco-leather portfolio with a lock, and carefully put the key in the left-hand pocket of his smoking-jacket.

He lunched. He even lunched well, for Eurtrude was what one familiarly calls a cordon bleu. Then he drank a Surat-mocha, while sipping a chartreuse and combusting the cylinder of a highly-priced cigar. The pleasure of all these things and the satisfaction of work well done was even tempting him into a pleasurable somnolence when a ring at the bell caused Eurtrude to walk in the direction of the front door. Even he started.

Enter Eurtrude, greatly excited.

EURTRUDE Monsieur, it's the gendarmes.

HUBERT How very extraordinary. What do they want with me?

EURTRUDE I don't know, Monsieur, I'm all of a tizzy.

HUBERT I shall receive them.

He adopts a dignified attitude.

'Show them in,' says he.

Enter the gendarmes.

HUBERT Messieurs.

GENDARMES (standing to attention and saluting him). Monsieur.

HUBERT(cordially) To what do I owe this honour?

FIRST GENDARME Does a man name of Icarus live here?

HUBERT Er . . . yes . . .

FIRST GENDARME He hasn't appeared before the Recruiting Board. He is therefore considered to be a deserter and we've come to march him off to the Reuilly barracks, where he'll be taken on the strength and brought to trial, before being sent to do his military service – in the African Battalion, perhaps.

HUBERT How awful!

SECOND GENDARME Here are his joining instructions. He's to come with us at once.

HUBERT Messieurs . . . I accept sole responsibility . . . I'd never thought about his military service . . . and then, a Recruiting Board scene in the novel I am engaged on would seem extremely vulgar and naturalistic.

FIRST GENDARME It's not a question of a novel, but of reality.

SECOND GENDARME And there's no getting away from that.

HUBERT Couldn't the matter rest in abeyance for a day or two . . .

FIRST GENDARME A thousand regrets. The law's the law.

HUBERT (overwhelmed). I'll go and get him for you.

He goes into his study, opens his morocco-bound file, and comes back with Icarus.

HUBERT Icarus, my dear fellow, I had forgotten to tell you that you are of an age to do your military service, and these gentlemen have come to fetch you. You must leave at once.

ICARUS You see, Monsieur, it didn't do you any good to bring me back here by force. I'm free again, now.

FIRST GENDARME Free, that's just a manner of speaking, because you've got to come with us.

ICARUS And where to, Monsieur?

SECOND GENDARME To the Reuilly barracks, where they'll consider your case, after which you'll do your time.

ICARUS What time?

FIRST GENDARME Your military service time.

ICARUS And how long will that be?

SECOND GENDARME Three years.

HUBERT So it is! Three years! Shall I have to wait three years to finish my book.?

FIRST GENDARME Monsieur, that is none of our business. (To Icarus), Come with us.

ICARUS I shall be only too pleased to come with you.

(To Hubert). I have nothing against you, but I'm going for a walk.

They go out.

HUBERT What a profession! What a profession!

XXXIV

At Surget's. The gendarmes take off their big false moustaches.

ICARUS Were you in disguise, then?

JACQUES I am not particularly fond of that expression, but in fact, yes: we were in disguise.

JEAN What an adventure! but we've got him.

SURGET (to Icarus). Make yourself at home. Sit down. We're going to ask you a few questions.

JACQUES Are you going to be the interrogator?

SURGET If you have no objection.

ICARUS May I ask you, gentlemen, who you are, and what you want of me?

SURGET You can't ask questions and be questioned at the same time.

JACQUES Be interrogated would be more accurate.

JEAN Let's not squabble.

SURGET Your name is Icarus, is it not?

ICARUS Yes, but that doesn't tell me who you are.

SURGET We are friends. Have we not delivered you from your master and tyrant?

ICARUS I didn't ask you for anything.

JACQUES That's true.

JEAN We're straying.

SURGET You're twenty, are you?

ICARUS And I won't have to do my military service?

JACQUES Not unless some real gendarmes appear . . .

SURGET Let's not jest. (To Icarus) Make yourself comfortable. Here, have a partagas. Would you like a finger of port wine?

ICARUS With pleasure.

SURGET Here you are.

JACQUES But why don't we let him speak?

JEAN Just to see.

ICARUS I really would like to know, gentlemen, who you are.

JACQUES That's of no importance.

ICARUS What's going to become of me?

JEAN That depends on what you tell us.

SURGET Naturally, I'm not going to interrogate you, but you're going to tell us . . .

ICARUS What?

SURGET Anything.

ICARUS But before that, gentlemen, may I not know who you are?

JACQUES What an obstinate fellow.

JEAN He's giving us quite some trouble.

SURGET Was it such a good idea? I wonder. And my scratch is beginning to itch again.

JACQUES Mine too — it starts itching every so often.

JEAN You're fine ones to talk.

SURGET Are your scars beautiful?

JEAN They call mine a trifle.

JACQUES Mine — I consider mauve.

ICARUS I'm just beginning to understand — you must forgive me for being so slow — you are the three musketeers with whom M. Lubert crossed swords in the Bois de Boulogne?

JACQUES So you read the gazettes?

ICARUS Now and then. By the way, could I please go and do pipi?

SURGET Most certainly; I even have a real English water closet.

(He shows Icarus to the w.c. and comes back).
Well, what do you think?

JACQUES I think the joke has gone on long enough. And anyway, there's no question of my using him. Not mauve enough.

JEAN Too naive for me.

SURGET I admit I don't understand him very well.

JACQUES Let's take him back to his place of origin, then.

JEAN Lubert must be foaming at the mouth. He'll make up his mind to go to the Reuilly barracks, and he won't find anyone.

JACQUES We must give him back before.

SURGET It'll just have been an innocent little practical joke, that's all.

JACQUES I say, he takes his time pissing, our Icarus.

JEAN You don't think . . .

SURGET There's only a narrow fanlight that gives on to

a little courtyard . . .

JACQUES Even so. I'm beginning to get worried. You ought to go and see.

SURGET It's rather embarrassing . . .

JEAN Oh, go on!

Surget goes on.
Comes back.

SURGET I knocked. He doesn't answer.

JEAN Perhaps he's fainted. Emotions.

SURGET It's locked, we'll have to send for a locksmith.

He sends for a locksmith.
The w.c. door is opened. No one.

JEAN We're in a fine mess now.

JACQUES Disagreeable surprise.

JEAN This time, Hubert will kill us.

JACQUES If he discovers that it was we . . .

SURGET I can see only one solution.

THE OTHERS What?

SURGET Morcol!

XXXV

ICARUS What am I afraid of? How can I hide? What will become of me? Everything is urging me towards the Avenue de la Grande-Armée, where I could develop my taste for the sports of cycling and automobilism. Those devilish bikes, those chuff-chuffing meteors, are leading my soul on towards Progress. A fig for the neurasthenias, the neuroses and the nostalgias of our contemporary writers! Forward into the future! What did M. Lubert want of me? Did he want me to drag out a melancholy existence, strewn with dismal or disappointing love-affairs, with sessions in cosy, dusty apartments where, biting my nails, I should have meditated on my soul which, if he'd dared, would have been an infanta in full regalia? I might perhaps have fought duels, but I should have been more likely to go wandering along by Italian lakes in the shade of chlorotic cypresses. Whereas personally, I'm much more interested in theoretical mechanics, from the fall of heavy bodies to the mechanism of a lock. What shall I do? Yes, everything attracts me to the Avenue de la Grande-Armée, hard by the Bois de Boulogne, where I got trapped by that tricky lady and that artful detective. It's true that M. Lubert must think I'm at the Reuilly barracks. Have those fellows admitted to their theft and my new flight? I've no idea, but no one will think I'm so stupid as to return to the district where I got caught. Let's go back there, then, and I might even find work there, because LN's spondulics will soon be exhausted, on account of her long absence which grieves me sorely.

He sets off in the direction of the Avenue de la Grand-Armée.

A mechanic was fiddling with the engine of an automobile. Icarus went up to him.

'Have you got a job for me, by any chance?' he asked him.

'Do you know the trade?'

'I can learn. I've often watched these machines going by'.

'Can you ride a bicycle?'

'No, Monsieur. No one ever taught me.'

'Well! Start with the bicycle, and then you can come and see me about the automobile.'

'But, Monsieur, how could I learn to ride a bicycle?'

'There's a school at the corner of the rue Belidor.'

'Do you have to pay?'

'Of course.'

'I shan't have any money left if I spend it there.'

'That's for you to decide.'

Icarus decides. He learns to ride a bicycle.

XXXVI

Hubert was smoking a partagas and thinking of ways and means to continue his novel: he might perhaps devote a few extra pages to Maîtretout and his daughter Adelaide, but after that he wasn't going to twiddle his thumbs for the next three years. He was contemplating some other solution, then, when the doorbell rang. Ah yes – he was expecting Mme de Champvaux for the adulterous hour. He goes to open the door. A coachman is silhouetted in the doorway.

COACHMAN Well, guv, what would you say to a few lashes of the whip?

HUBERT Oh no, darling, believe me: I'm really not the least bit interested in the whip. I'm not a sadist.

COACHMAN (correcting him). A masochist.

HUBERT We aren't going to squabble over a question of significs! Come in!

The coachman comes in and cracks his whip. He takes off his hat, and of course it's none other than Mme de Champvaux.

Mme DE CHAMPVAUX Do you still like me dressing up as a jehu?

HUBERT Believe me, you're imagining things. Just because I once . . .

Mme DE CHAMPVAUX Yes, but it did revive your ardour.

HUBERT Listen, I just don't know what you ought to

112

be dressed up as today. I've got things on my mind again.

Mme DE CHAMPVAUX You mean I'm casting my pearls before swine?

HUBERT I'm afraid so, my love. Just think — Icarus has been taken away by the gendarmes.

Mme DE CHAMPVAUX What for?

HUBERT His military service. It had never crossed my mind.

Mme DE CHAMPVAUX And how long will this comedy last?

HUBERT Three years.

Mme DE CHAMPVAUX You mean you'll be in this state for three years?

HUBERT Perhaps longer, if he has to do extra time.

Mme DE CHAMPVAUX Well — when things begin to look up, you can let me know. Fat lot of use it was me putting on my boots and Inverness cape.

Exit, cracking her whip.
Hubert absent-mindedly sips a finger of port wine.

HUBERT (suddenly, striking his forehead). Why don't I quite simply go to the Reuilly barracks?

XXXVII

SURGET (to the other two). No need for you to come up with me — I'll take charge of everything. See you tonight, my friends.

Surget stops at the door: the name is inscribed on an enamelled plate. A venomously nauseating corridor leads to a similar type of staircase.
Surget pulls a cord. A bell rings.

MORCOL Monsieur: I am at your disposition.

SURGET Mine is a very unusual case.

MORCOL All cases are unusual, Monsieur.

SURGET And mine, particularly so.

MORCOL Delighted to hear it.

SURGET This case is all the more unusual in that you have already dealt with it.

MORCOL Pff!

SURGET I've come about Icarus.

MORCOL You aren't M. Lubert.

SURGET Obviously not. My name is Surget. Just think, I'd pinched Icarus from him . . .

MORCOL After I took him back? Well — obviously.

SURGET Two of my friends and I, we kidnapped him. Why? — it would be complicated to tell you why. In short, we kidnapped him. But no sooner had we kidnapped him than he took wing. We would very much like to find him, to give him back to Lubert. We thought of you — you did so well the first time. Why not the second?

MORCOL Why not? But I shall charge you more.

SURGET Divided by three, it still won't come to very much. So go to it! With all your strength. I'll give you the necessary details.

XXXVIII

At Hubert's, during his absence.

MAITRETOUT You mustn't cry like that. The boy's doing his military service. Every Frenchman. It's his duty. Obviously a duty is a duty, but, well, military service has its good points, you get a breath of fresh air, you take some exercise, you make friends, you might even get promotion.

ADELAIDE (sniffing). Even so, it was very unexpected. Who could have expected it? Even M. Lubert himself didn't expect it. He was going to marry us in a month. If he'd foreseen this military service, he wouldn't have arranged for us to be married in a month.

MAITRETOUT M. Lubert knows more about these things than we do.

ADELAIDE Oh, but of course!

MAITRETOUT Come come, my child, cheer up, and have confidence in M. Lubert.

ADELAIDE He's broken my heart. Three years is a long time. Icarus will forget me: he'll prefer any camp-follower or soldier's doxy to me.

MAITRETOUT Why do you think he'll be so fickle?

ADELAIDE L'uomo è mobile . . .

MAITRETOUT What do you know about it, my poor child? — you're barely twenty pages old.

ADELAIDE But I have the wisdom of the heart, even if

116

I haven't any experience.

MAITRETOUT While we're waiting, just to pass the time, let's have a game of backgammon — even though you do always win.

ADELAIDE Because I'm unlucky in love, my sweet Papa.

XXXIX

HUBERT Oh, Doctor, I've suffered a new misfortune.

DOCTOR Icarus?

HUBERT We can't find him! I've looked for him in vain at Reuilly. Unknown on the muster-roll, if that's what you call it. No one knows who those gendarmes were. There's a mystery, here, whose heart cannot be plucked out. In short, Icarus has disappeared again: it's enough to make one quite neurotic.

DOCTOR The moment you have a reason, it's not called neurotic any more. And anyway, diagnosis isn't your business, it's mine.

HUBERT And then, I'm lacking in ardour. Mme de Champvaux will insist on dressing up as a coachman to stimulate my imagination, but personally it doesn't amuse me at all, oh but not at all, oh dear, *not at all*.

DOCTOR Calm down.

HUBERT Easy to say.

DOCTOR Supposing you never find your Icarus.

HUBERT Unthinkable! I *must* find him! And anyway, I've got Morcol on the job again . . .

DOCTOR He might not manage it, this time.

HUBERT No, he'll pull it off again.

DOCTOR If he doesn't, you'll just have to make the best of it.

HUBERT I'm not going to make the best of it. This novel can't remain unfinished.

DOCTOR It won't be the first.

HUBERT You talk about it very lightly.

DOCTOR Write something else, damn it! You have more than one string to your bow.

HUBERT For the moment, it's this particular one I want to shoot with, and none other.

DOCTOR You're obstinate. Here — come and lie down on the couch.

HUBERT What for? Are you going to give me an injection?

DOCTOR No, no. Here. Just lie down. (Hubert reluctantly lies down). That's it — good — I sit behind you, and you tell me everything that comes into your head.

HUBERT What's the point? What's the good of that?

DOCTOR It's a new method of psychotherapy for neuroses.

HUBERT The mysterious new method that's superseded bicarbonate of soda? You seem to think I'm a guinea-pig. A neurotic guinea-pig.

DOCTOR Come on: lie down.

HUBERT (querulously). What d'you want me to tell you? I tell you everything as it is.

DOCTOR Well, but now, don't tell me anything, just talk. Say anything — no matter how trivial.

HUBERT (indignant). But I never say anything trivial. I know what I mean and I mean what I say. Trivial, indeed! Do you want me to lower my standards?

DOCTOR Adopt a middle course. Tell me a dream.

HUBERT A dream . . . a dream . . . that's different. I'm very much in favour of dreams, though I never use them in my literary work.

DOCTOR Lie down, then, and tell me one.

HUBERT (suddenly jumping up). Next time. Next time. I've got to go and have a dream, first. And if you think *that's* so easy . . .

XL

MORCOL (sitting on a bank of the Seine, watching the water flow by).

I'm in a Corneillian situation. M. Lubert has once again engaged me to find Icarus, a mission with which M. Surget has also entrusted me. If I find Icarus, to whom shall I return him? This seems to be a question of conscience, but in the meantime I have a foot, as they say, in both camps. I went to the Globe and Two Worlds Tavern which he used to frequent in the days when I'd got his name wrong, but he hasn't been back there, any more than has the little grisette I saw him with at the Café Anglais. He hasn't been seen at the Café Anglais either, and I had enough trouble finding even that out. As a criminal always returns to the scene of his crime, and even though Icarus cannot be considered, even in the strictest sense, to be a criminal, I can see no other trail than the Bois de Boulogne where he jumped so courageously, a courage that was perhaps unconscious, at the head of Mme de Champvaux's horses, of which act the lady then came to inform me, and make the bargain which enabled me to return the fugitive to M. Lubert's pages. Yes, the Bois de Boulogne seems indicated for my preliminary research, even though it is fairly extensive, 872 hectares, if I have been accurately informed.

XLI

ICARUS (on his bicycle. He is dressed in the appropriate fashion for such a situation and, what's more, he's wearing an automobilist's cap and goggles).

I feel I'm becoming a poet
astride on my bike — watch me go it!
I'm singing and writing a song
as I weave in and out of the throng.
Though clutching my handlebars tight,
seat on saddle — I feel I'm in flight!
The passers-by get so irate —
but it's splendid, it's gorgeous, it's great!

Oh, sorry Monsieur.

Still singing he rides on.

MORCOL Clumsy oaf! I was in a very dangerous situation, there. I'm quite upset. I can't even remember why I'm in the Bois de Boulogne. Let me think . . . Ah yes. Well, even so, there's not much point in trying to run after him.

122

XLII

Now that he could ride a bicycle and pump up a tyre, Icarus, as his nest-egg had vanished, was engaged by M. Berrrier, mechanic, automobilist, garage-owner and repairer. So Icarus learnt to drive an automobile carriage. He went pop-popping down the Avenue de la Grande-Armée, it was delightful. Since he had become an autodidact he was earning money, and in the evenings he would dine alone, and very respectably, in an out of the way restaurant; a different one every evening.

M. BERRRIER Everything all right, then?

ICARUS Yes, Monsieur.

M. BERRRIER You know, your work's very satisfactory, but there's one thing that worries me – you always seem to be looking over your shoulder. You haven't got a crime on your conscience, have you?

ICARUS No, Monsieur.

M. BERRRIER All the same, you do seem suspicious. I've been watching you – you always look this way and that before you put your nose outside. Are you afraid of someone, or what?

ICARUS I'm not afraid of anything, Monsieur Berrrier. Only I sometimes say to myself: if there's a bit of a draught – you never know – I might take wing.

M. BERRRIER. What an idiot you are, Icarus!

XLIII

ADELAIDE My sweet Papa, I've made up my mind: I'm going to look for him.

MAITRETOUT What are you saying? What are you going to do?

ADELAIDE Go to him! Find him!

MAITRETOUT You? A pure young girl! Plunge into such an adventure! Over my dead body!

ADELAIDE Come with me then, Father!

MAITRETOUT You want us to abandon this abode where we're so nice and warm, this novel where we're so well nourished, and our kind M. Lubert?

ADELAIDE Our kind M. Lubert! Too bad for him. He should have taken better care of Icarus. Let's run away.

MAITRETOUT What can I say? What can I do? I can't let you wander alone in this vast Paris.

ADELAIDE You see! Let's fly! He hasn't closed his manuscript; let's take advantage of this opportunity.

MAITRETOUT It breaks my heart. Leaving poor M. Lubert and his water-marked paper!

XLIV

SURGET Well, Morcol, your enquiry doesn't seem to be getting anywhere and it's beginning to cost us a lot of money. Aren't you on his trail?

MORCOL The Bois de Boulogne. Everything leads me back there. Reason, flair, intuition, not to mention my method of free association — everything sends me in that direction. Unfortunately the Bois de Boulogne is vast; what's more, it's dangerous. You keep nearly getting run over.

SURGET What does that matter! Go back there! Sleep there! Camp there!

MORCOL Hm, that's all very well, Monsieur, but I tell you, with all these new vehicles, it's very dangerous.

SURGET We'll increase the fee! But get on with it!

MORCOL I'll be risking my life.

SURGET I'll double your fee.

MORCOL All right, then: after all, there's the country air.

XLV

MORCOL As I said to M. Surget, everything leads me back to this wood where rustic birds used to sing in former days, but which is now becoming a race-course for automobile monsters.

DE DION-BOUTON (charging at him). Vrrrt! Vroom! Vrrrt!

MORCOL (dodging). Him again! He's definitely just thrown himself into my arms, as it were! Not without risks to my person, professional risks, you'll say, quite so, but that's not the point.

A bird sings

MORCOL (thoughtfully) All this needs some consideration.

XLVI

Icarus sat down on a bench and watched the sparrows pulling at bits of grass and bickering. He wasn't thinking of anything when a solemn-looking gentleman in a top hat sat down beside him. The gentleman took a bag out of the pocket of his tail-coat, dug into it and started throwing seed to the little birds who gathered round for the feast. When he's emptied his bag, the gentleman rolls it up in a ball and puts it back in his pocket though the feathered fraternity did not immediately disperse, as they still had some hope of a supplementary ration. The gentleman then lights a modest cigar with all the usual precautions, sends several puffs up to the heavens and, turning to Icarus, says:

'You see, I'm rewarding myself. Something for the little birds, something for myself.'

ICARUS Yes, Monsieur.

THE GENTLEMAN Aren't you going to give the little birds anything?

ICARUS The idea hadn't occurred to me; I thought they managed by themselves. To tell you the truth, I'd never actually thought about it at all.

THE GENTLEMAN Have you thought about other problems?

ICARUS The problem of the automobile, for instance. I'm in the trade. A new form of motion . . .

THE GENTLEMAN You move with your times, I see.

ICARUS Very funny.

THE GENTLEMAN I didn't do it on purpose; but perhaps you are surprised at my speaking to you? Perhaps you think I'm indiscreet?

ICARUS Far from me, such a thought.

THE GENTLEMAN Or do you take me for a paederast?

ICARUS What's a paederast?

THE GENTLEMAN Sancta simplicitas, let's forget it. To tell you the truth, if I spoke to you it was because I feel you are a confrère . . . a colleague . . .

ICARUS Are you interested in automobile carriages, too?

THE GENTLEMAN In no way.

ICARUS I can ride a bicycle, as well.

THE GENTLEMAN No no, it's not that. I was talking about your mode of existence.

ICARUS It's simple.

THE GENTLEMAN I suspect you . . .

ICARUS (getting up). You're mistaken!

He runs away.
The gentleman has got up, too, and he runs after Icarus. He soon catches him up. He gallops along, side by side with Icarus, who can't outrun him. As if they were running on the spot.

THE GENTLEMAN Don't be afraid! I don't wish you any harm.

They continue to run on the spot.
Thus Icarus finds himself on an identical bench with the gentleman at his side.

THE GENTLEMAN I knew it. You're sitting on this bench because you're running away from the Bench.

ICARUS The fact is . . . How did you guess?

THE GENTLEMAN I'm in the same situation.

ICARUS I thought mine was unique.

THE GENTLEMAN People always think that, but actually we're never alone. I too, Monsieur, I left the writer who set me down in writing, for that is the situation you are in, is it not?

ICARUS Yes, Monsieur.

THE GENTLEMAN It's mine, too.

ICARUS And what's your author called?

THE GENTLEMAN Surget.

ICARUS I know him. He's a friend of *my* author. He played a dirty trick on him and filched me, but he didn't keep me long.

THE GENTLEMAN I didn't know. That must have been before I existed. Such as you see me now, Monsieur, I'm only about ten days old: yes, Monsieur, about ten days old. M. Surget started me about ten days ago and you can see how old I am. He gave me quite a respectable past. Born in Rodez on the 18th of April 1855, I went to the Lycée in Cahors where I did well, and then to the Lycée in Orléans, where I lost my meridional accent. I got a second class honours Arts degree, after which I started my career as a draftsman in a Ministry where I performed wonders because in due time I became chief clerk. So far, you will say, there has been nothing particularly extraordinary, but the plot thickened when I got married. When I *was* married, rather, and I won't spell out for you who was responsible for my marriage. He married me to a horrible woman, a lustful shrew, a poisonous adulteress. She deceives me. Yes, Monsieur, she deceives me. This leaves me totally indifferent, but here's where things begin to get nasty. M. Surget was trying to incite me to crime. He led up to it very gently and then one fine day — if that's what you can call it — I was supposed to make cold meat of her — yes, that's a pretty apt expression because I was supposed to chop her up with a chopper, something pretty sordid. Hold hard! I said: Nothing doing. In the first place, it's a procedure I disapprove of: you don't kill a woman even if she does get on your nerves; and then, you never know where it may lead. I have no wish to mount the scaffold with a view to seeing my head tumble into the bran basket. So I packed up bag and baggage, and here I am feeding the sparrows, a taste for which I am indebted to M. Surget.

ICARUS Have you been gone long?

THE GENTLEMAN Only since this morning.

ICARUS What are you going to do?

THE GENTLEMAN Go back to the Ministry.

ICARUS M. Surget will nab you there.

THE GENTLEMAN I hadn't thought of that.

ICARUS Not to speak of Morcol, who's bound to be on your trail.

THE GENTLEMAN Morcol?

ICARUS A detective who specialises in shadowing people. He's after me. He caught me once, but I got away.

THE GENTLEMAN Then I ought not to go back to my Ministry?

ICARUS I wouldn't advise it.

THE GENTLEMAN That's all very fine, but . . . where am I going to live? to sleep? to get some money? to eat? I hadn't thought of all that.

ICARUS I can get you a job at my garage. What can you do?

THE GENTLEMAN I can cook. I'm a dab hand at it, and M. Surget never even knew.

130

XLVII

MAITRETOUT My child, I'm hungry!

ADELAIDE My sweet Papa, I've broken into my piggy-bank and I've brought the money in my purse. We'll go to a restaurant and you can cheer yourself up by consuming some nourishing food.

MAITRETOUT Isn't it foolhardy to eat that money?

ADELAIDE No, my sweet Papa. Thanks to my feminine intuition and to the inspiration of love, it won't be long until we find Icarus, I'll marry him, because no sooner said than done, and we'll go back to live with M. Lubert, who's sure to have a splendid future in store for me, and a wise old age for you, my sweet Papa. So we can spend the money I've brought quite shamelessly, even though prudently.

MAITRETOUT I'm dying of hunger, I can't bear it any longer, I'm not getting any younger. My child — let's find a tavern as soon as possible.

ADELAIDE (firmly) No, my sweet Papa, we won't go to a tavern, but to a Duval Restaurant.

They go into a Duval Restaurant. They eat there. Adelaide checks the bill and pays it in very small small change, in sous.

MAITRETOUT What are we going to do now, my child — now that we're refreshed?

ADELAIDE We're going to look for Icarus, my sweet Papa! We're going to look for Icarus.

XLVIII

HUBERT Good evening, Eurtrude. Is there any news?

EURTRUDE None at all, my good master.

HUBERT No express letters? No visiting cards?

EURTRUDE Neither nor.

HUBERT Well then, Eurtrude, bring me a finger of port wine and some biscuits which I shall eat with a view to cheering myself up. After which, I shall do a bit of work.

Eurtrude obeyed and Hubert did as he had said. Having eaten a few biscuits he sat down at his work table.

HUBERT Yes, I shall carry on with the book I started. True, Icarus is missing, but while I'm waiting for him to come back I shall force myself to return to some of the minor characters and devote to them the several pages which, according to my plan, are their due. This is the result of Dr. Lajoie's advice: it is so good that I am following it; on the other hand I don't for a moment doubt that Morcol will discover Icarus in next to no time. He trapped him once, didn't he? Bis repetita placent. No reason why he shouldn't find him again: I'll elaborate the character of Maîtretout, then, and bring his daughter more into focus. Maîtretout, in spite of his name, only teaches symbolist poetry; it's true that this is not lacking in secrets: vowel colour, consonant flavour, subtle hypallages – the whole alchemy of words. Maîtretout, in short, is a modern Faust. I'll get him to say a few words.

Silence.

132

HUBERT What? What's that I hear? Nothing! Maîtretout, Maîtretout, where are you? No funny business, eh?
You aren't going to disappear too, are you? Anyway, you
wouldn't leave your daughter all alone. Would he, Adelaide? What? What's that? What's that I don't hear?
Adelaide! you aren't going to disappear too, are you!
Adelaide! Mademoiselle! Ah! the little wretch! She's
disappeared with her Papa!

He rings a hand bell.

EURTRUDE You rang, Monsieur?

HUBERT Eurtrude, you haven't seen anyone leaving
here, have you?

EURTRUDE No one, my good master.

HUBERT Nor coming in? Any gendarmes, for instance?

EURTRUDE Absolutely nothing, my good master,
absolutely nothing.

HUBERT Gendarmes, in fact — an absurd hypothesis.
Eurtrude! give me just a finger of port wine, and I'll have
some biscuits with it. (Alone). This is becoming farcical!
All the same, my characters can't just decamp like that,
one after the other. What have I got left, in fact? Just the
foot-sloggers. Shall I be able to carry on with these other
ranks?

XLIX

SURGET (wiping his mouth) That was an excellent dinner that you concocted, my good lady. I shall go and work, now. My man is waiting for me. Adultery has been committed. He discovers it. You can guess what follows: he avenges his honour but, and this is the point: not honourably, in a distinguished manner, with a pistol, for example, but bestially, with appalling cruelty.

Mme SURGET What a black soul you have.

SURGET My man is going to kill his wife with a chopper. I'm even wondering whether I won't make him make mincemeat of her.

Mme SURGET How horrible!

SURGET Like the legend of Saint Nicholas.

Mme SURGET Well, if it relieves your feelings!

SURGET Give me, my wife and spouse, a finger of port wine, and then I'll start.

He drinks his finger of port wine and sits down at his work table.

SURGET My character, I forgot to tell my wife and spouse, is named Corentin Durendal, a name which I had great difficulty in finding. Durendal is obviously an allusion to the fatal chopper and Corentin stresses his Breton origin; born in Rodez, his parents came from Morbihan: this is the sort of thing that novel readers are interested in. Corentin Durendal, that peaceable civil servant, is preparing to commit a crime, but for the moment, as is his wont, he is feeding the birds, just like a Racinian Eternal Father. I see encircling him all that little twittering, feathered world, innocent and volatile, who have not the slightest suspicion that their peaceable foster-father is about to commit an atrocious crime. I see, then, Corentin Du . . . no, though, I don't see him. And yet he hadn't finished feeding the little birds! Maybe he's changed benches. No, though. All the benches are empty, except the one occupied by a couple of lovers.

THE COUPLE OF LOVERS We're kissing because we were told to kiss.

SURGET Those two must come from Jean.

In any case they disappear, as Jean has moved them to the Bois de Vincennes.

SURGET No more Corentin! No more Durendal! It's not possible! No, it's not possible! I don't understand. But, but, but . . . could the peaceable Corentin Durendal have played the same trick on me as Icarus did to Lubert? It's astounding! Corentine! Corentine!

Mme SURGET (coming running). Did you call me, my treasure?

SURGET Corentin Durendal, the hero of my novel, the one I was telling you about just now, the one who was going to kill his wife with a chopper — Corentin Durendal has disappeared!

Mme SURGET Ah, the good fellow!

SURGET So that's how you share my distress.

Mme SURGET Oh but I do, my treasure, I do, I do share it, but I also understand perfectly that M. Corentin Durendal should refuse to kill his wife. Especially with a chopper.

SURGET My stick! my hat! I'm going to see Morcol! He'll find him for me. Recourse to him is my only

135

resource.

Mme SURGET Believe me, my treasure, all you have to do is not make him kill his wife, and M. Corentin Durendal will come back.

SURGET No, no! I want him to kill her. Thanks for the stick, thanks for the hat! I'm going to see Morcol. I shall run all the way!

L

The Globe and Two Worlds Tavern.
Enter LN

THE DRINKERS 'But it's LN!'
'LN! What's become of you?'
'What had become of her?'
'LN! LN! but it's LN!'
'What's become of you, LN?'
'What had become of her?'

LN Greetings, Messieurs.

WAITER (coming running). Yes, Madame?

LN A round for everyone!

THE DRINKERS Hurrah for LN!

FIRST DRINKER So you're back! We haven't seen you for such a long time.

LN I've changed my beat.

SECOND DRINKER And what good wind brings you back here?

LN I wanted to see my old friends.

FIRST DRINKER That was nice.

WAITER Here are the absinthes.

LN This will be the last glass of wormwood I shall drink here.

SECOND DRINKER You just wanted to see us again, and that's all?

137

WAITER See us again, and that's all?

LN See you again, and say adieu! Adieu to my past life, to my somewhat frivolous youth! Allow me to inform you, dear absinthe drinkers, that I am abandoning my former profession and setting up as a dressmaker.

FIRST DRINKER How banal!

LN Far from it! For I shall neither sew nor make ordinary clothes, but solely bloomers for lady bicyclists. I am setting up near the Avenue de la Grande-Armée and the Porte Maillot, the district in which our modern means of transport are coming into being.

SECOND DRINKER You're moving with the times, LN, and even faster than them.

LN That's just what I think. The bicycle is not only going to start a new fashion, it will also give our sedentary peoples a taste for travel and tourism; it will revive our dormant provinces, attract visitors to the country, facilitate human relations among villagers not merely in the same parish but even in neighbouring parishes, and finally it will give the Frenchwoman the liberty her Anglo-Saxon sisters have already conquered. This is what people are saying, and I proclaim it.

ALL THE DRINKERS Bravo! Hurrah for the Bike! Hurrah for Sport!

They drink their absinthes.

LI

MORCOL (in his office). I don't know why I am so possessed by melancholy since the sylvan walks to which the exercise of my profession leads me, walks which however are disturbed by the modernity of the character I am supposed to be following. Melancholy, blissful melancholy, you incite me to retire from this story. I want to relax, to take my modest savings and go to the Riviera to breathe the balmy effluvia of the orange and lemon trees. Yes, that's where I shall go and live. It's a sudden decision, but it's already quite firm. We shall abide by it, and it's just too bad for our clients:

A bell rings.

MORCOL But there's the bell. Who can be coming thus to trouble me in my sonorous meditations?

He goes to open the door.

SURGET Ah! my dear man!

MORCOL He calls me my dear man!

SURGET (very emotionally) My dear man!

MORCOL Things must be going badly.

SURGET Give up the search for Icarus . . .

MORCOL I already have.

SURGET And find me Corentin Durendal.

MORCOL One of your characters?

SURGET Yes. I've just noticed that he's disappeared. So you see, Icarus is only of secondary importance, now. You must get on Durendal's trail. And anyway, I don't think you'll have any difficulty; he's a peaceable civil servant, you'll easily pick up his tracks.

MORCOL Monsieur Surget, you're wasting your breath.

SURGET What does that mean?

MORCOL I'm giving up, Monsieur Surget. I'm giving up. No more shadowing. And above all, no more shadowing of shadows — meaning the insubstantial images of authors' imaginations. Monsieur Surget, I'm shutting up shop.

SURGET You can't do that to me!

MORCOL That's the way it is.

SURGET My fortune! my fortune for Durendal!

MORCOL Not for a billion francs.

SURGET Just once more! One last time!

MORCOL I am neither a puppet nor a marionette. Nothing can make me go back on my decision.

SURGET You have no pity.

MORCOL I have some for myself.

SURGET You wouldn't allow my quill to run dry over a work that would have been embellished by an abominable crime?

MORCOL To wit?

SURGET With a chopper.

MORCOL Banal.

SURGET Not in the eyes of my public. What a novel it would make!

MORCOL You'll write others. That's what I always told M. Lubert.

SURGET And you're going to leave him too without his Icarus?

MORCOL I tell you, I'm shutting up shop, I'm packing my bags, and I'm off to the shores of the Riviera to breathe the balmy effluvia of the orange and lemon trees.

SURGET Then I will leave you, alas, cruel Morcol, prostrate with grief. It's my punishment: I steal Icarus, and Corentin Durendal steals away.

MORCOL Maybe, but I'm off.

LII

Doctor Lajoie prescribes a little bicarbonate of soda.

'Is that all, Doctor?' asks the sufferer. 'I've heard that antipyrine . . . or Pink Pills . . .'

'Well well! so that's where we've got with popular medicine and the pharmaceutical advertisements which are displayed not insidiously but in abundance in the daily and even weekly papers. So that's where we've got: the patient wants to heal himself! Any minute now he'll be wanting to write out his own prescription!'

'Then, Doctor, you think . . .'

'Bicarbonate of soda is a miracle medicine which, in moderate doses, will do you the greatest good. Drink a little herb tea as well, but not to excess'.

When the valetudinarian had gone, Doctor Lajoie went to check that there was no one left in the waiting-room. He was sure there wasn't, but being of an anxious temperament he needed to make assurance doubly sure. Having gone round his consulting room in a clockwise direction, and then in the opposite direction, he half-opened the door and saw Surget.

DOCTOR You here! I didn't hear you come in.

SURGET As no one opened the door, I pulled the catch and that loosed the latch.

DOCTOR My housekeeper has gone to consult a healer in the provinces and her substitute leaves at five o'clock, but that can't be of any special interest to you. What ill wind brings you here?

SURGET As the saying goes, I don't know which way to turn.

DOCTOR Sit down, my dear friend. I'm listening.

SURGET Have you cured Hubert Lubert?

DOCTOR I flatter myself that I have! While he's waiting for Icarus to come back he's continuing his novel with some of his minor characters: this is one of my greatest successes. I've cured him so thoroughly that I don't see him any more, which causes me a certain loss of revenue. But that is a matter of minor consequence to me. Have you ever reflected, my dear friend, on this paradox? If doctors had not sworn to be authentic disciples of Hippocrates, would it not be in their interest to make their cures last as long as possible?

SURGET Excuse me, Doctor, but your problems are for the moment of little comfort to me: I would prefer to tell you about *my* problems. Or rather, my problem.

DOCTOR My digression was provoked by your question: 'Have you cured Hubert Lubert?', you know. But go on: I'm listening.

SURGET Well, the same thing has happened to me. My chief character has disappeared.

DOCTOR Get Morcol to look for him.

SURGET As the saying goes: hic jacet lepus. He doesn't want to work any more. It's a veritable catastrophe.

DOCTOR Not really. He hasn't found Icarus — why do you suppose he'd be any more likely to find yours?

SURGET How true; I hadn't thought of that. What a marvellous thing common sense is. As the saying goes: it's the commonest thing in the world.

DOCTOR Yes: except there's also such a thing as being on short commons.

SURGET Meaning that *I* am short of common sense? Would that be your opinion, Doctor?

DOCTOR Not at all, not at all.

SURGET Thank you. What do you advise me to do, then?

DOCTOR Imitate your colleague Hubert Lubert. Continue the same novel with the other characters, or else start another one.

SURGET It's idiotic, your advice.

DOCTOR It's common sense speaking through my mouth. This said — would you like me to convince you of it by a suitable form of treatment?

SURGET What sort of treatment?

DOCTOR You lie down on that couch and tell me everything that comes into your head.

SURGET That's not my style, saying whatever comes into my head. I know what I mean, when I say something, and I mean what I say. Say whatever comes into my head, indeed!

DOCTOR Well, tell me a dream, then . . .

SURGET They're idiotic, dreams. And anyway, I never dream. As the saying goes, I've put all my imagination into my novels, and nothing into my dreams.

DOCTOR A missed opportunity, then: an act of omission.

SURGET Stealing Icarus didn't bring me luck.

DOCTOR We protoanalysts don't call that an act of omission. It's a failed act of commission.

SURGET And what does the vocable 'protoanalyst' signify?

DOCTOR That significant designates a new profession which I am adding to that of sawbones which has so far been my only signification. And thanks to my practice of this profession I am now in a position to help you in one way or another in your search, but to that end you must lie down on this couch.

SURGET Just a moment! As the saying goes: time is money — so give me some money to think.

LIII

LN had set up shop at No. 5 rue Belidor. Here she employed three young shop-ladies. The workshop opened on to the courtyard; its all-female staff consisted of two bloomer-makers, one alteration hand and three apprentices. So it was quite a little business that LN had drummed up and she was certainly to be seen in two if not three places at once, receiving the clients, presiding at fittings and supervising the production. In short, she was doing a roaring trade. LN was in the money, and she could easily have supported Icarus if he, for his part, had not received some slight pecuniaries through making himself useful to M. Berrrier.

LN had taken so kindly to commerce that one might almost have thought she had been born to it. One day, for example, in comes a woman, what may I do for you, Madame?, such are the words pronounced by LN, and the woman answers, I'd like some cycling bloomers, something very smart. You've come to the right shop, Madame, LN tells her, I have the very thing to adorn the posterior and accentuate the calves. Here, Madame, is the very latest model, one of my personal creations, in Scottish tartan with longitudinal gussets, perfection itself, which will fit you like a glove, especially in view of the way Madame is built, absolutely made for you, you'll be delighted, just come this way, Madame, and let us try it on you. Once we've removed the frills and furbelows you'll see for yourself, Madame, that these bloomers, a model of my personal creation in Scottish tartan and with longitudinal gussets, that these bloomers fit you with miraculous ease and that thus bedizened you really look like a goddess. In the Miss Velocipede competition you will certainly bear the palm, like Hera on Mount Ida.

THE CLIENT I thought it was Aphrodite.

LN Just a rumour. In any case, what does classical mythology matter. What counts for us women is modern mythology, the Fairy Electricity, the Eiffel Tower, the Panhard-Levassor and the little queen, as we up-to-date French call the bicycle. And of all the queens who ride the little queen you, Madame, as I have already remarked, will be the goddess. You have already made your decision, I am sure, there is no need for me to press the point, will you take it with you?

THE CLIENT No; I want it delivered.

LN Name? Address?

THE CLIENT Madame de Champvaux, 130 rue La Boétie. Cash on delivery.

She goes out.

LN Strange fate that brings us face to face. Could it be a trap? A Macchiavellian plot?

LIV

At the garage. Corentin Durendal is cautiously dusting a new automobile with a clean cloth.

MONSIEUR BERRRIER Well, Icarus, what do you say to this little jewel?

ICARUS I say: phew!

MONSIEUR BERRRIER It's a Panhard-Levassor. They'll be able to get up to twenty miles an hour with this. Maybe even twenty-two or twenty-three.

ICARUS But where will people go, to drive at such speeds? It's hopeless in the Bois now, it's full of forest-rangers.

MONSIEUR BERRRIER They'll have to build a special road where there'll be nothing but automobile carriages. They'll call it an autodrome.

ICARUS What a dream! Speed without forest-rangers.

MONSIEUR BERRRIER Well, yes. But the trouble is that on such an autodrome people would be going from nowhere to nowhere.

ICARUS But why, Monsieur Berrrier, would people be going from nowhere to nowhere?

MONSIEUR BERRRIER Because the autodrome, by definition, would be circular.

ICARUS I don't see why. Neither auto nor drome prescribe circularity, according to the distant and instinctive remembrance I still have of the tongue of my

147

ancestors.

MONSIEUR BERRRIER Perhaps not. But personally I see it as circular: I have a perfect right to, haven't I?

ICARUS I won't contradict you, Monsieur Berrrier.

MONSIEUR BERRRIER An even madder dream would be a road solely reserved for automobiles, which would go from somewhere to somewhere.

ICARUS And that would be called an autostrada.

MONSIEUR BERRRIER No, an autoroute.

ICARUS Right, Monsieur Berrrier.

MONSIEUR BERRRIER A still madder dream is when there won't be any more automobile carriages at all. They'll have disappeared like the mammoth. And we mechanics and garage men will be a forgotten species, like the species of marine animals whose fossilised traces are found in Kimmeridge clay, for instance.

ICARUS You at least, Monsieur Berrrier, take the long view. You're a real prophet.

MONSIEUR BERRRIER Let's not exaggerate.

ICARUS But it's true, Monsieur Berrier; only very few people can see into the future like you can.

MONSIEUR BERRRIER I must admit that . . .

ICARUS Well then tell me, Monsieur Berrrier, do you believe that one day people will be able to do something like sixty miles an hour?

MONSIEUR BERRRIER Never, my boy. Never.

LV

EURTRUDE Is that you Monsieur Morcol? The master has been waiting for you most impatiently.

MORCOL He's going to be disappointed.

He goes into Hubert's study.

HUBERT Ah, there you are. Did you get my express letter?

MORCOL The reason for my visit.

HUBERT Have you found Icarus?

MORCOL No.

HUBERT Well, you'll have to add Maîtretout and his daughter Adelaide to the list. They've flown too, but as I presume that Adelaide is trying to find Icarus, that should give you a clue. Or even a clew. You'll catch all three of them; it must be easier to find a community than an isolated individual.

MORCOL How long have they been gone?

HUBERT Four days. I might have told you earlier, I agree. I must admit that I was hoping they'd come back of their own accord, and perhaps even bring Icarus with them.

MORCOL Monsieur Lubert, I regret to have to inform you that I'm shutting up shop.

HUBERT I beg your pardon?

MORCOL I say, I'm shutting up shop. I am no longer practising as a detective.

HUBERT But then . . . Icarus . . . Maîtretout . . .
Adelaide . . . Can I no longer place any hope in you?

MORCOL None.

HUBERT And what about the advances I gave you?

MORCOL You'll have to write them off.

HUBERT But that's fraud! both economical and
psychological.

MORCOL I'm declaring myself bankrupt.

HUBERT No more help from you? Come come, just a
little effort. You managed to find Icarus for me once, you
can equally well manage it again, and all the more so as I'm
giving you a new lead.

MORCOL No argufying, Monsieur Lubert. I'm giving
up. I am going to retire to the shores of the Riviera to
breathe the balmy effluvia of the orange and lemon trees.
And do you know how I intend to go there?

HUBERT What do I care.

MORCOL By bicycle.

LVI

At the Club.

JACQUES My dear man, I have some serious news to tell you.

JEAN So have I.

JACQUES Chamissac-Piéplu has disappeared.

JEAN So have *all* my characters! A whole file of them. I haven't a single one left. Isn't it mad?

JACQUES Who would have thought it of him?

JEAN Just one, well all right, but all of them at the same time! Even the minor characters! even the concierge's parrot.

JACQUES Chamissac-Piéplu was a gilded youth. Money — women — he had everything!

JEAN What a mess we're in.

JACQUES We might perhaps ask that detective to help us . . .

SURGET (insurgent) My friends, I have some painful news to tell you. Corentin Durendal has disappeared.

JEAN AND JACQUES We're all in the same situation.

SURGET You too?

JEAN AND JACQUES We too! Deprived of our creations! Our only hope now is you and Morcol.

SURGET My friends, what a sad disappointment is in

151

store for you! Morcol no longer wishes to engage in this sort of business!

JEAN Catastrophic!

JACQUES Decidedly, the situation is mauve.

SURGET Ah! if we hadn't stolen Icarus, this would never have happened to us.

JEAN AND JACQUES We don't see the connection.

LVII

LN Careful! She'll soon be here to fetch her cycling bloomers.

ICARUS The only thing she ever seems to think of is dressing up.

LN My cycling bloomers are most becoming.

ICARUS I think they're hideous, and the women who wear them look like silly geese.

LN Don't disparage my trade.

ICARUS It's not your trade I'm disparaging, it's the fashion. I hope you're not going to start wearing them, to set the example.

LN Seeing that I don't ride a bicycle. It's the automobile for me. Thanks to you.

ICARUS The bicycle is a thing of the past.

LN In the meantime, the little queen is all the rage, and riding a bike in bloomers of LN's creation, well, my clients think that's fine.

ICARUS All right, I didn't say a thing. I'm going to work, now.

LN As I said before: be on your guard against la Champvaux.

ICARUS I'll be on my guard — but she must have forgotten me, you know.

LN No one ever forgets you.

LVIII

The Berrrier garage. M. Berrrier is from home. Icarus has taken the Panhard-Levassor out to give it a breath of fresh air. Corentin Durendal, alone, is leaning on a broom, dreaming. A young lady arrives, carrying a suitcase. Which she puts down. She is accompanied by a silent chaperon.

THE YOUNG LADY Anyone there?

CORENTIN DURENDAL (slowly raises his eyes, and says nothing).

THE YOUNG LADY Anyone in?

CORENTIN DURENDAL (slowly lowers his eyes, and says nothing).

THE YOUNG LADY Anyone around?

CORENTIN DURENDAL (slowly raises his eyes and says nothing).

THE YOUNG LADY Not even an echo?

CORENTIN DURENDAL Corentin Durendal.

THE YOUNG LADY And Papa?

CORENTIN DURENDAL I haven't the honour of the acquaintance of your respected father.

THE YOUNG LADY M. Berrrier, of course.

CORENTIN DURENDAL In that case, it is his garage I have the honour to sweep, and his tyres — or rather those of his automobiles — that I have the honour to dust.

Mlle BERRRIER Isn't he here?

CORENTIN DURENDAL No, Mademoiselle. Not for an hour.

Mlle BERRRIER Drat. An hour. What am I going to do while I'm waiting?
(Turning to his silent companion): What am I going to do while I'm waiting?

SILENT CHAPERON (raises her eyes to heaven).

Mlle BERRRIER I'm going to sit down.

CORENTIN DURENDAL (pointing to a de Dion-Bouton). Sit in there. With Madame. You'll see how comfortable it is.

Mlle BERRRIER I don't dare, it might start all by itself.

CORENTIN DURENDAL You've nothing to be afraid of. It's so difficult to start that it needs both the strength of a grown man and the skill of a mechanic.

Mlle BERRRIER (to her silent chaperon). Shall we try?

SILENT CHAPERON (lowers her eyes to the ground).

Mlle BERRRIER (climbing up to the seat in the de Dion-Bouton). This is the first time I've ever been in an automobile. Very interesting.

SILENT CHAPERON (sits down in the car without manifesting any emotion either one way or the other).

Mlle BERRRIER And does it go?

CORENTIN DURENDAL With this machine you can go much faster than a galloping horse.

Mlle BERRRIER What a galley-yarn.

CORENTIN DURENDAL In no wise, Mademoiselle. It's the honest truth. When M. Icarus is driving he goes even faster than your father.

Mlle BERRRIER Who's M. Icarus?

155

CORENTIN DURENDAL A mechanic who works for your father. A most talented young man. Almost an engineer.

Mlle BERRRIER Is he handsome?

CORENTIN DURENDAL He's a magnificent young man.

Mlle BERRRIER I love him already! (to her silent chaperon). And I shall marry him.

SILENT CHAPERON (raises her eyes to heaven).

156

LIX

MAITRETOUT I'm getting tired. We've nearly got to the Porte Maillot and we've been walking for over an hour.

ADELAIDE Well, my sweet Papa — look at that bench, which is holding out its arms to you. Let's sit down.

MAITRETOUT Let's sit down!

They sit down.
Silence.

MAITRETOUT (suddenly). Adelaide, look! but look!

ADELAIDE But at whom, my sweet Papa?

MAITRETOUT At that man there, in front of us, sweeping out that garage.

ADELAIDE Yes, my sweet Papa, I can see him quite well. He's working conscientiously.

MAITRETOUT Don't you notice anything?

ADELAIDE No, my sweet Papa. I think I can guess that the gentleman hasn't always been a sweeper, that he has known better days, that . . . ah! my sweet Papa, I'm beginning to see what you mean . . .

MAITRETOUT I mean that . . .

ADELAIDE He's like us . . .

MAITRETOUT Yes (pause). Let's go and put the question to him, tactfully, even though I am so extremely tired.

They get up and go over to Corentin Durendal.

157

MAITRETOUT Excuse me, Monsieur.

CORENTIN DURENDAL Monsieur . . .

MAITRETOUT Could you kindly tell me the way to the Porte Maillot?

CORENTIN DURENDAL Monsieur, you're practically there. Just a few more steps in that direction (gesture).

MAITRETOUT You must excuse me . . . but when one doesn't know Paris . . .

CORENTIN DURENDAL So Monsieur and Mademoiselle come from the provinces? That's no disgrace.

MAITRETOUT Of course it isn't! All the more so as we come from even farther away, if I may so put it.

CORENTIN DURENDAL Might you be foreigners?

MAITRETOUT In a certain sense. Like you yourself I believe, Monsieur.

CORENTIN DURENDAL What does that mean?

MAITRETOUT I shall perhaps not surprise you when I tell you that I was born when I was fifty years old, and that even though I was born at that age I already had a daughter of eighteen. Hadn't I, my child?

ADELAIDE Yes, my sweet Papa.

CORENTIN DURENDAL It doesn't surprise me.

MAITRETOUT You yourself, Monsieur . . .

CORENTIN DURENDAL I am forty years old, and have existed for a week.

MAITRETOUT That's just what I thought . . . you were born, like me . . . like her . . . at the tip of a quill. . .

CORENTIN DURENDAL I guessed it the moment I saw you.

MAITRETOUT So did I.

CORENTIN DURENDAL Since you are in the same situation as I, you must be on your guard.

MAITRETOUT Against whom?

CORENTIN DURENDAL Against a certain Morcol . . . he's looking for us all . . . he's looking for me, he's looking for Icarus.

ADELAIDE Icarus! Do you know him?

CORENTIN DURENDAL Indeed I do! He works here.

ADELAIDE Oh God! (she faints in her father's arms.)

LX

DOCTOR I assure you that if you could just tell me about some little act of omission, you'd feel much better.

HUBERT I don't write plays.

DOCTOR I don't understand.

HUBERT If I wrote plays, even if I wrote one with only one act, it wouldn't mean that I'd omitted the others.

DOCTOR I meant in everyday life. Don't you ever forget your keys? don't you ever have a lapse of memory? miss a train? find yourself on the wrong floor?

HUBERT Not so far as my recollection goes. That I am mad, 'tis not true.

DOCTOR It's not a question of madness. We proto-analysts start in this way because you are averse to free association and you never seem to dream.

HUBERT I find all your prototypal practices extremely displeasing, Doctor. It only remains for me now to pay you and go home.

DOCTOR It's the paying that counts; you'll see how much good it'll do you.

Hubert pays and leaves.
He goes home and sits down at his table on which is placed a blank sheet of paper. He looks at it for a long time in silence.

HUBERT And anyway, to blazes with them all! They can go where they like, all the Icaruses, Maîtretouts and Adelaides. I'm going to start another novel!

He dips his quill in the ink and starts to write another novel.

LXI

EURTRUDE Monsieur! Here's another shrovetide reveller!

Mme DE CHAMPVAUX (in cycling bloomers) (she comes sailing in). How do I look?

HUBERT Whatever next.

Mme DE CHAMPVAUX Is that all you can find to say to me?

EURTRUDE Personally, I am gone with the wind.

She disappears.

Mme DE CHAMPVAUX What an idiot she is. And you just sit there gaping!

HUBERT Er . . .

Mme DE CHAMPVAUX No doubt about it; all I get from you is suspicion and incomprehension.

HUBERT Well, you know me . . . out-and-out modernism . . .

Mme DE CHAMPVAUX What a let-down.

Silence.

Mme DE CHAMPVAUX (resolutely) if that's how it is, I'll take them off.

HUBERT No no, not now. I'm working.

Mme DE CHAMPBAUX You're working! Is Icarus back?

HUBERT No, but I'm writing another novel.

Mme DE CHAMPVAUX Then you've got your ardour back?

HUBERT My ardour for work.

Mme DE CHAMPVAUX All I can do now, then, is go and get some more cycling bloomers made.

LXII

CORENTIN DURENDAL Lunch is ready!

ICARUS Aren't we going to wait for M. Berrrier?

CORENTIN DURENDAL He's taken his daughter out to a restaurant to celebrate her return.

ICARUS Has he a daughter?

CORENTIN DURENDAL Yes. And his daughter has a chaperon.

ICARUS That's news to me. Why have you laid four places, then?

CORENTIN DURENDAL We have guests.

ICARUS *I* haven't invited anybody.

CORENTIN DURENDAL You'll see. Come in!

(Enter Maîtretout and Adelaide).

ICARUS So we meet again!

ADELAIDE You aren't particularly surprised?

ICARUS Not really.

CORENTIN DURENDAL Lunch is ready!

MAITRETOUT Your welcome seems a bit callous, to me, Icarus.

ICARUS I'll soften it. Why don't we have an absinthe?

MAITRETOUT I never touch it: it's poison.

CORENTIN DURENDAL (opens a bottle of red wine

and pours it out all round. He gets them to pass the sardines-in-pure-olive-oil).

They're Amieux sardines. I took them out of the tin myself.

ICARUS So, Monsieur Maître tout, you've been following me?

MAITRETOUT It's rather that I've been following my daughter.

ICARUS Weren't you happy at M. Lubert's?

ADELAIDE My timidity, and the proprieties, forbid me to answer that, without you, I was unhappy there.

CORENTIN DURENDAL It's touching. M. Surget would never have thought of that. All he knew about was adultery.

MAITRETOUT Shh! In front of a young lady . . .

ADELAIDE My sweet Papa, I know what it is. I know life, now, since I've been roving through this vast Paris looking for . . . Monsieur.

ICARUS In my day, it wasn't the young ladies who declared themselves to the young men.

ADELAIDE It can be read in modern novels.

ICARUS Oh, I'm more read about than a reader.

ADELAIDE We were destined to understand each other.

MAITRETOUT I approve, I approve this badinage, but I deplore the fact that it is taking place over sardines at the back of a garage. You must resume your tender banter in some bosky wood — or wait till the next full moon.

ICARUS You're right, Monsieur Maître tout; let's change the subject. Let's come back to you, Monsieur Maître tout. You really have nothing to reproach M. Lubert for, apart, if I may so put it, from Adelaide being crossed in love.

ADELAIDE I'd like some more sardines.

164

MAITRETOUT I even thought M. Lubert extremely likeable. He had great qualities, and he'd endowed me with some considerable ones. The only thing I disapproved of, and I imagine that you share my opinion on the matter, was his liaison with Mme de Champvaux.

ICARUS (absent-mindedly). She had some cycling bloomers made.

ADELAIDE A madwoman.

ICARUS A scheming hussy. I am as much afraid of her as I am of Morcol.

CORENTIN DURENDAL Don't let's talk about them, that's the best thing. Or we might attract them like a magnet attracts iron shavings.

ADELAIDE Iron filings.

CORENTIN DURENDAL And do you know M. Surget, Monsieur Maîtretout?

MAITRETOUT I saw him two or three times at M. Lubert's. I wouldn't want to have anything to do with him.

ICARUS I agree with you. He had me kidnapped by bogus gendarmes. Luckily I got out of his clutches.

CORENTIN DURENDAL And what about me? He had prepared an extremely distasteful fate for me.

MAITRETOUT Might one know what fate?

CORENTIN DURENDAL I was supposed to kill my wife with a chopper.

ADELAIDE How frightful!

CORENTIN DURENDAL And now I'll bring you the steak and chips, it's my speciality. Nice and rare.

LXIII

CORENTIN DURENDAL Monsieur Maîtretout – a liqueur?

MAITRETOUT Well, I really believe I will. You are an exquisite cook. What a good lunch, and it's a pleasure to be amongst our own kind.

ICARUS What do you mean by that, Monsieur Maîtretout?

MAITRETOUT I mean, amongst our own kind . . . you know what I mean.

ICARUS Do you feel different from the other men in the street?

MAITRETOUT Yes . . . even though, amongst them there may well be some . . . like us . . . you know what I mean.

ICARUS Well personally, Monsieur Maîtretout, I don't see the slightest difference. You, Lubert, Morcol, Mme de Champvaux and Adelaide – for me it's the same thing.

MAITRETOUT Even so . . . even so . . .

ICARUS Once we are free, don't we have the same desires, the same needs? The same faculties? Don't we have to obey the same necessities of life?

MAITRETOUT Once we're free, yes, but we always run the risk of returning to a different state if we're caught. The other men in the street don't.

ICARUS How do we know? It may all come to the same

thing. They may be the characters of some other sort of author.

MAITRETOUT There, I can't follow you.

A voice calls into the garage: Anyone there?

ICARUS I'll go.

He knocks back his liqueur and goes.

A YOUNG FOP Young man, I should like to buy forthwith and for cash an automobile that travels with the greatest possible rapidity.

ICARUS Monsieur, the boss isn't here yet, he'll be back any minute now. In the meantime I can show you one or two models ... To tell you the truth, the only ones we have left for sale are this de Dion-Bouton and that Panhard-Levassor. They can both reach a maximum speed of nearly thirty miles an hour.

THE YOUNG FOP How can I choose?

ICARUS They are both equally strongly built and they are exactly the same price.

THE YOUNG FOP Which is ...?

ICARUS Thirteen hundred and ninety-five francs.

THE YOUNG FOP Here it is.

He puts the money down somewhere: on a work-bench, for instance.

ICARUS Without the boss, I can't sell you ...

THE YOUNG FOP I'm in a hurry.

ICARUS I'm sorry.

THE YOUNG FOP (peering at Icarus). Young man, I seem to know your face.

ICARUS And I ditto your ditto.

THE YOUNG FOP I seem to recognise you and to remember the place we met, but all this seems extremely extraordinary and extraordinarily unlikely.

ICARUS Yes, it was indeed I, Monsieur, whom you challenged to a duel at the Café Anglais.

CHAMISSAC-PIEPLU A mechanic! frequenting the Café Anglais!

ICARUS I wasn't a grease monkey in those days.

CHAMISSAC-PIEPLU This duel in abeyance ...

ICARUS Oh, personally, you know, I don't really set so much store by it.

CHAMISSAC-PIEPLU Well, neither do I. I'm in a great hurry and, if I may say so, I have other fish to fry. What's more, given the singular circumstances during the course of which we made, if I may so put it, each other's acquaintance, and which give me to think that we must have something in common, I'll tell you a secret.

ICARUS I can guess it.

CHAMISSAC-PIEPLU Then I won't tell you.

ICARUS There's no need. Leave your money there for the boss of this garage and take one of these two automobiles. You'll soon be out of sight.

CHAMISSAC-PIEPLU Young mechanic, you're a friend.

He climbs up into the seat of the de Dion-Bouton.

ICARUS By the way, though — can you drive?

CHAMISSAC-PIEPLU M. Jacques arranged for me to take lessons. He'll wish he hadn't!

DE DION-BOUTON Vrrrt! Vroom! Vrrt! Vroom!

CHAMISSAC-PIEPLU Adieu!

He disappears.

168

LXIV

BALBINE Then it's settled, Father? I can marry M. Icarus?

MONSIEUR BERRRIER I've nothing against it, but at least wait until you've met him.

BALBINE My mind is made up.

MONSIEUR BERRRIER In any case, in less than a minute you'll know where you are ... There he is. He's bending over the engine of the Panhard-Levassor.

BALBINE For the moment, all I can see is his behind. I like it.

MONSIEUR BERRRIER But ... the de Dion-Bouton's gone! Icarus! Where's the de Dion-Bouton?

ICARUS I've sold it, Monsieur Berrrier.

MONSIEUR BERRRIER My de Dion-Bouton! I loved it!

ICARUS So did I, but wasn't it for sale?

MONSIEUR BERRRIER Alas, yes. So you've sold it. Who to?

ICARUS I can't remember his name.

MONSIEUR BERRRIER What about the documents?

ICARUS We didn't bother with such details — but here's the money.

MONSIEUR BERRRIER It's quite correct. Right. And now, Balbine, let me introduce my right hand, Icarus.

ICARUS Mademoiselle.

BALBINE Monsieur.

MONSIEUR BERRRIER (to Balbine) Shall I tell him everything?

BALBINE Oh yes, Father.

MONSIEUR BERRRIER You haven't changed your mind?

BALBINE Oh no, Father.

MONSIEUR BERRRIER Well, Icarus, in less time than you'd think possible, you're going to become my son-in-law.

ICARUS With Mademoiselle?

MONSIEUR BERRRIER Don't tell me that this calls for reflection. She has a nice little nest-egg, a dowry in pneumatic tyres and accumulators and, apart from all that, she's a pretty little creature, isn't she?

ICARUS The thing is, I'm already engaged.

BALBINE Oh God! (she faints in her father's arms).

ICARUS Only I don't particularly want to marry my fiancée, alas.

BALBINE (coming out of her coma). Heaven be praised!

ICARUS But I've got what they call a mistress.

MONSIEUR BERRRIER A liaison. They're made to be broken.

ICARUS And there's a society lady chasing me.

BALBINE Monsieur is very much in demand.

ICARUS So you see, it really does call for reflection. Monsieur Berrrier — couldn't we talk about it some other time?

BALBINE If that's the way it is, I'm off to visit the Eiffel Tower.

She signals to her chaperon.

MONSIEUR BERRRIER Take a fly!

They go.

MONSIEUR BERRRIER Icarus, Icarus, I believe my Balbine is very angry with you. You mustn't hurt her.

ICARUS What about the others?

MONSIEUR BERRRIER My first thoughts are for my daughter — that's natural, isn't it?

ICARUS While we're waiting to solve this question, I'd like to ask you, M. Berrrier, whether you might not have another job for another friend of mine?

MONSIEUR BERRRIER Another Corentin?

ICARUS A very scholarly man, a professor of symbolist poetry. He could write you some leaflets in heptasyllables.

MONSIEUR BERRRIER What an idea.

ICARUS He'd make a good impression in this decor. He has a certain majesty.

MONSIEUR BERRRIER You're trying to turn my garage into a waxworks.

ICARUS He could talk elegantly to your upper-class customers.

MONSIEUR BERRRIER Where is he?

ICARUS I sent him for a walk with his daughter.

MONSIEUR BERRRIER And do I have to take on the daughter, as well?

ICARUS The daughter, Adelaide, is none other than the fiancée I was just telling you about.

MONSIEUR BERRRIER But Balbine . . .

ICARUS Not a word to Balbine. I'll find Adelaide a job somewhere else.

MONSIEUR BERRRIER I really don't know whether I ought to hope to have you for a son-in-law or not.

ICARUS You can't possibly know. I'll bring you Maîtretout at a time . . .

MONSIEUR BERRRIER Maître Two-at-a-time . . .? Is that his name?

ICARUS I didn't invent it.

LXV

ICARUS (singing softly).
The athlete takes precautions
Performing his contortions
For any great distortions . . .

He interrupted his efforts, as the only other more or less
perfect rhyme that sprang immediately to his mind was
abortions, and he couldn't see how he could insinuate this
word into his little song, even though M. Maîtretout had
taught him that he could quite well use less perfect rhymes
such as exertions, or allowable ones such as dissipations, or
even assonances such as patience or, still more surprisingly,
end his lines with words like halberd or misericord. He
stopped short and started to examine his surroundings,
whereupon he saw some kids playing with a kite. This
object had not so far played any part in his experiences; he
took a lively interest in it. It was an extremely ordinary
kite with a long tail adorned with paper frills, for which
Icarus could not see any explanation. It, the kite, was
flying quite high in the sky, the child holding it on a leash
was running hither and thither, and the air-borne rhomb
was following the erratic movements imposed upon it by
the wind and the fantasy of its puerile guide. Icarus
admired the simplicity of this ingenious machine, the
elegance of the aerial movement and the ceruleanity of the
atmosphere. He stayed there until the game was over.

Then he went back to town.

LXVI

ICARUS Adelaide, you must understand that your sweet Papa, notwithstanding his eminent qualities, won't earn a great deal of money in his new profession. And so as not to be a burden to him, you'll have to earn your living. Which is not the fate that M. Lubert had in mind for you for he, if I remember rightly, was going to provide you with a leisurely existence, and the hope that it would last for a long time. But you can still think better of your actions and, if you don't like the idea of working, go back to M. Lubert.

ADELAIDE I don't want to go back to M. Lubert.

ICARUS In that case, we'll have to find you a profession.

ADELAIDE I am very willing, but profession have I none. I am a well brought-up young lady who knows how to play the piano, paint in watercolours, sew a fine seam . . .

ICARUS Sew — that's it. Come with me, Adelaide, I'll find work for those fairy fingers of yours.

They walk a few steps and come to LN's boutique. They enter.

LN Ah! good day Monsieur Icarus! this must be the young person of whom you spoke?

ICARUS It is indeed, Mademoiselle LN. She is called Adelaide, sews a fine seam and has fairy fingers.

LN Perfect! Marvellous! I have the very thing for her.

174

Does that suit you, Mademoiselle — bloomers-maker?

ADELAIDE (blushing). *Che sara, sara.* I will bloomerise, Mademoiselle (she starts crying. Icarus proffers a chair, on which she collapses, sobbing).

LN to ICARUS Quick, get going: Mme de Champvaux will be here any minute. She's always ordering bloomers.

Icarus disappears.

ADELAIDE (through her tears). Where is my enchanted youth? Where the happy fate for which I was destined? Love caused me to flee the pages that had become nothing more for me than absence and desolation, and I am now reduced to utilising my fairy fingers on tasks of which I shall be ashamed, and which may well give me naughty thoughts.

LN There are no foolish trades, and there's nothing to be ashamed of. In any case, we only work for ladies. We make cycling, and feminine, bloomers.

ADELAIDE I shall get used to it.

MADAME DE CHAMPVAUX (coming sailing in). Well, my new bloomers? Are they ready? These cycling bloomers are marvels, even though they don't produce *all* the expected results.

LXVII

ICARUS Did you admire the beauties of the capital, Mademoiselle?

BALBINE Call me Balbine.

ICARUS Did you admire the beauties of the capital, Balbine?

BALBINE You're a cad, Icarus.

ICARUS I see you don't appreciate the delicacy of my sentiments.

BALBINE (to her chaperon). Disappear, chaperon!

(The chaperon disappears).

(to Icarus). You're a cad to refuse the future ownership of this garage, which will inevitably expand with the progress of automobilism. Be reasonable, Icarus: marry me.

ICARUS Your arguments, Balbine, do not impress me: I don't so specially believe in the progress of automobilism.

BALBINE That verges on the paradoxical.

ICARUS For me, the future is in the air.

BALBINE Another paradox.

ICARUS Since the surface of the earth is limited, saturation point will be reached, one day. Take the streets of Paris, for example: it isn't possible for more than so many carriages to circulate in them. After which — that's the end. There's even a speed limit. Everything is limited.

Whereas the air and the atmosphere have much more space to offer. Before flying vehicles congest the heavens . . .

BALBINE But there *aren't* any flying vehicles. Well — a balloon or two . . . but that's nothing . . .

ICARUS There soon will be.

BALBINE In the meantime: marry me.

ICARUS Let's not talk about the garage, then.

BALBINE I'm very willing to talk about other things.

ICARUS I'm listening.

BALBINE Icarus — do you know what I'd like? I'd like us to be the hero and heroine of a romantic novel.

ICARUS Out of the question.

BALBINE (all ears). Have you had an unhappy love affair?

ICARUS That isn't what I mean. On the contrary — a very happy one, but that's not all there is to . . .

BALBINE To what?

ADELAIDE (calling from outside). Icarus!

ICARUS Coming!

BALBINE And who might that be?

ADELAIDE (coming in and pointing to Balbine). And who might that be?

ICARUS (introducing them). Adelaide . . . Mademoiselle Berrrier . . .

ADELAIDE She's after you.

BALBINE What vulgarity!

ADELAIDE I wasn't speaking to you.

BALBINE So I should hope.

177

ADELAIDE Pretentious creature.

Balbine slaps her face.
Adelaide kicks her in the tibias.
Balbine slaps her face again.
Adelaide grabs a can of oil and pours its contents over
Balbine's head.

MONSIEUR BERRRIER (coming up). Wretch! What
are you doing to my daughter? to my beloved daughter?

ADELAIDE What a laugh. Ha ha.

MONSIEUR BERRRIER My poor child. (to Icarus).
And you allow this person to have her way? After I took
you in, you, and not only you, but all these bizarre
creatures who have come and agglomerated themselves
around your person! Out, everyone! Out, Icarus! and
that's my final word.

LXVIII

Morcol gets off his bike and goes into LN's shop.

MORCOL Madame, I am preparing for a long journey which will lead me to the shores of the Riviera, there to breathe the balmy effluvia, and to this end I have acquired a bicycle and learnt to use it. I can ride quite well, now. So all I need is the costume ad hoc, which is why I have come to this shop to buy some cycling knickerbockers and some tight stockings, as well as a cap and other ingredients.

LN I'm sorry, Monsieur, but we only make clothes for ladies.

MORCOL How extremely distressing. But now I come to think of it, Madame, haven't I met you before somewhere?

LN Hell!

MORCOL You are the young person who . . .

LN You must be mistaken.

MORCOL Not that it matters, though, for . . .

ICARUS (coming in). (he pays no attention to Morcol. To LN). I'm out of work! M. Berrrier has turned us all out! Icarus, he said . . .

LN Whatever are you saying? . . .

MORCOL You too, Monsieur, I recognise you . . . and I observe now that you are precisely one metre 76 and that you are called Icarus. As for me, I am Morcol, ex-private detective. Don't worry, your fate doesn't concern me any

179

more. I'm only thinking about my own, now. I am retiring from business and going by bike to the shores of the Riviera to breathe the balmy effluvia of the orange and lemon trees. And so, Madame, you haven't any cycling knickerbockers for gentlemen?

LN No, Monsieur, I'm sorry.

MORCOL Well, adieu then. Monsieur Icarus, I shall at least have found you! What a consolation for my amour-propre, and what a satisfaction for my old age!

LXIX

ICARUS Right: so I'm rid of poor Adelaide: she's accompanying M. Maîtretout into exile, and he's following Corentin Durendal en route for a fate which he hopes will be different. They are disappearing from my ken. As for me, kept by the cycling bloomers trade and LN's love; I go back to the fortifications every day and there examine, rather than the Apaches and Jezebels sleeping in the close-cropped grass, and there examine, I say, always with the same interest, the children's game that consists in making paper rhombs, known as kites, sway in the breeze. Now that I am excluded from the cycling and automobile industry, I dream of a destiny which I can only vaguely foresee and of which M. Lubert has, no doubt, not the slightest inkling. M. Lubert, poor M. Lubert, now his detective has abandoned him he must be terribly bored without me and with no hope of ever seeing me again. M. Lubert, poor M. Lubert, a generous gesture would be . . . The only thing I don't like about kites is the string that curbs them . . . M. Lubert, poor M. Lubert, a generous gesture would be . . .

LXX

EURTRUDE Monsieur, Icarus is at the door. He would like to speak to you.

HUBERT Icarus. Which Icarus? Ah! Icarus? Is he there? Show him in, then.

Icarus appears. His attitude is modest.

HUBERT Icarus, my dear fellow! So here you are! How are you? Sit down! you must tell me all about it.

ICARUS (sitting down on the edge of a chair). Yes, Monsieur.

HUBERT I'm listening, Icarus. A partagas? A finger of port wine?

ICARUS (with a gesture of refusal). No thank you, Monsieur.

HUBERT Go on then, my dear fellow. I'm listening.

ICARUS Monsieur Lubert, I haven't come to tell you my adventures — you can hear about them later, if you like — but to make you a proposition.

HUBERT I am more and more attentive.

ICARUS A proposition that has some conditions attached.

HUBERT Conditions? Let's hear them: this seems curious.

ICARUS Well then. If you are willing to take back with me a person in whom I have the most lively interest, I am ready to return to your work. Obviously the very fact of the existence of this person would considerably modify the plot of your novel, for you would no longer dispose of either M. Maîtretout or Mlle. Adelaide, who have gone their way, and who have been followed by Corentin Durendal, who has not the same origin as we.

HUBERT I know. He's one of Surget's.

ICARUS You might perhaps be able to do without them.

HUBERT Well, my poor Icarus, none of this interests me in the slightest. But of course! — I wasn't going to spend my whole life getting people to look for you, especially as the best sleuth who specialises in that line has let me down and is leaving the profession.

ICARUS I know. I met him.

HUBERT (after a moment's surprise, continues). I wasn't going to get personally involved in the search, naturally enough. And I wasn't going to twiddle my thumbs and wait patiently till you came back. No, I've started another book which is going according to my wishes and, let me stress, with faithful characters. So you will understand, my poor Icarus, that I am not interested in your proposition.

ICARUS (standing up). Really not?

HUBERT Really not. I'm sorry, but I have no more use for your character.

ICARUS What I was saying, Monsieur Lubert, was for your benefit. Because personally, I've found my vocation.

HUBERT (holding out his hand). Everything's for the best, then! Good luck, Icarus.

ICARUS Thank you, Monsieur.

False exit.

ICARUS Wouldn't you like me to leave you my address? Just in case . . .

HUBERT Give it to Eurtrude! Give it to Eurtrude!

Exit Icarus.

HUBERT Even so, I'm touched by his visit. I wonder what on earth his vocation can be, I ought to have asked him. What does it matter, though.

He resumes his work.

LXXI

DOCTOR Hallo LN, I haven't seen you for ages.

LN You can call me Mademoiselle LN now, Doctor, because I'm a bloomer-maker.

DOCTOR There's no such thing as a foolish trade.

LN I didn't come to see you to talk about bloomers, nor to consult you on my behalf. It's about Icarus.

DOCTOR Aha!

LN He wanted to go back to M. Lubert. He told me that if M. Lubert took him back, he'd take me too. But I don't want to. It was a generous gesture on Icarus's part, but I don't want to become a character in a novel. My origin is quite different.

DOCTOR And what is it?

LN Cruciverbal.

DOCTOR Cruciverbal?

LN It's true, you couldn't understand. But I love Icarus, and this is the first time that anything has come between us.

DOCTOR If you are of different origins, perhaps your union would be ill-matched?

LN We understand each other perfectly. Except for this generous gesture. Couldn't you persuade M. Lubert to refuse? — that's what I've come to ask you.

DOCTOR Lubert is writing another novel. He *will* refuse.

LN It seems that he was so attached to Icarus.

DOCTOR All this is none of my business.

LN Won't *you* make a generous gesture, too?

DOCTOR I can't interfere, but I can make enquiries, and to that end I shall use that marvellous invention, the telephone.

LN The telephone!

DOCTOR (picking up the receiver). Hallo, hallo: Mademoiselle, will you please connect me with M. Lubert, who lives at 14 rue de La Rochefoucauld . . . I'll wait as long as is necessary, Mademoiselle . . . hallo hallo . . . hallo hallo . . . hallo hallo . . . ah, my dear Lubert . . . you haven't by any chance had a visit from . . .

NASAL VOICE From Icarus? How did you know?

DOCTOR . . . Er . . . just a rumour . . .

NASAL VOICE Well, Icarus has gone. I don't want any more to do with him. Aren't I right?

DOCTOR It's not for me to give you advice, but a little bicarbonate of soda wouldn't do you any harm.

Lubert hangs up. He can't be very pleased.

DOCTOR It looks as if your visit was unnecessary. You'll get your Icarus back.

LN Oh, thank you, Doctor. What do I owe you?

DOCTOR I'll make you a present of the telephone call. It'll be a wedding present.

LXXII

JEAN I found them all back in their places. I don't understand. Anyone might have thought I'd been seeing things.

JACQUES I've given Chamissac-Piéplu up as lost. But not the colour mauve. My Chamissac-Piéplu wasn't mauve enough. My new characters are so mauve that they'd never dare run away.

JEAN Ha, here's Surget. He looks radiant.

SURGET Ah, my friends, what a story! Do you want me to tell it to you? it'll interest you.

JEAN (to Jean), and JACQUES (to Jacques). We can guess.

SURGET Well, just imagine, I've found Corentin Durendal, my wandering civil servant. He repented of his ways. And better still: I've inherited two characters from a novel of Lubert's whom he had abandoned; a charming young lady, Mlle Adelaide, and her father, an eminent elderly professor, M. Maîtretout. I think I'll be able to make something of them.

JEAN What will Lubert say?

SURGET Nothing at all. I asked him. It's all the same to him. My goodness — I've adopted them.

JACQUES So you'll be able to make a fresh start, now?

SURGET Yes. I shall have to adapt the plot a little. Nothing serious. And then, I like this Mlle Adelaide, and I'm hoping to learn something from M. Maîtretout.

JEAN What does he teach?

SURGET Irregular rhetoric.

187

LXXIII

HUBERT Icarus's reappearance bothers me. Perhaps I was wrong to refuse his conditions. What I'd like to do now is go back to the novel I started with him, and finish it. And then, his vocation intrigues me.

Mme DE CHAMPVAUX Well then — accept his conditions.

HUBERT I'd already thought of that.

Mme DE CHAMPVAUX The fact that I've thought of it too doesn't make it a bad idea.

HUBERT I think, after all, that I will accept them.

Mme DE CHAMPVAUX But how are you going to find him, now?

HUBERT I have his address! Eurtrude! his address!

EURTRUDE Monsieur?

HUBERT Icarus's address!

EURTRUDE Just a moment, Monsieur, and I'll find it . . . 5 rue Belidor.

Mme DE CHAMPVAUX But that's the address of my bloomer-makers.

HUBERT That's highly suspicious. You want me to get Icarus back because . . . because . . . perhaps you're already his mistress?

Mme DE CHAMPVAUX I swear I'm not! It was for your own good that I said you should accept . . .

HUBERT My own good ... hm ... I've given up the idea of looking for Icarus.

Mme DE CHAMPVAUX Your jealousy verges on folly.

HUBERT Jealousy cannot be controlled.

Mme DE CHAMPVAUX I promise you ...

HUBERT Don't promise anything.

Mme DE CHAMPVAUX To prove to you the nobility of my feelings, so long as you work with Icarus, you shall see me no more.

Mme de Champvaux disappears abruptly.

HUBERT Now I am free from other preoccupations, let's come to a decision. (He thinks for a long time). This decision was already arrived at at the beginning of this chapter: let's lose no time in finding Icarus!

He is out in the street. An automobile taxi passes.

HUBERT Let us take advantage of the opportunity Progress offers us! Driver!

189

LXXIV

HUBERT (to Hubert in his taxi).
Here's number five in the rue Belidor. It is in fact a
cycling-bloomers shop. She wasn't lying. Let's go in.
(he goes in).
Might I speak to M. Icarus, please?

A SHOP GIRL M. Icarus has gone out with Madame.

HUBERT And might I know where they have gone? It's
very important.

THE SHOP GIRL They've gone to the ground.

HUBERT (aghast) To fight a duel?

THE SHOP GIRL Hee hee. No, to the ground where
they fly kites.

HUBERT They fly kites? And where is this ground?

THE SHOP GIRL Along the Seine, near the Puteaux
bridge.

HUBERT Thank you for that precious piece of inform-
ation.

He throws himself into his taxi and shouts out the
address.

THE TAXIDRIVER Ah, Monsieur wants to see the
cantharodrome?

HUBERT The cantharodrome? What's that?

THE TAXIDRIVER Hasn't Monsieur heard? It's in all
the papers, sometimes on the sports page and sometimes
on the science page.

190

HUBERT I so rarely read them. Just an occasional glance at the literary pages.

THE TAXIDRIVER Ah well, personally . . .

HUBERT Can't you go any faster?

THE TAXIDRIVER I've got my foot right down.

HUBERT And what might that mean?

THE TAXIDRIVER That I am pressing down the accelerator with all my strength.

HUBERT Ah . . . the accelerator.

A little further on, outside the cantharodrome.

THE TAXIDRIVER You're just in time: he's taking off.

Hubert leaps out of the taxi. Something is moving in the air. Down on the ground, the spectators are commenting on the events.

HUBERT Who is it? What is it? Anyone might think it was a man . . .

SPECTATOR It is.

HUBERT Who is it? Who is it?

SPECTATOR Icarus, of course. First flight with a passenger.

ANOTHER SPECTATOR A girl called LN.

ANOTHER SPECTATOR Icarus is gaining height.

ANOTHER SPECTATOR He's over the Seine, now.

ANOTHER SPECTATOR He's beating all the records.

ANOTHER SPECTATOR He's climbing!

ANOTHER SPECTATOR He's climbing!

ANOTHER SPECTATOR He's climbing!

ANOTHER SPECTATOR You can hardly see him.

191

ANOTHER SPECTATOR He's disappearing into the clouds!

ANOTHER SPECTATOR He's reappearing!

ANOTHER SPECTATOR He's climbing again!

ANOTHER SPECTATOR He's climbing too high! Something's going to happen to him.

ANOTHER SPECTATOR But ... but ... he's coming down again!

ANOTHER SPECTATOR He's not coming down: he's falling!

ALL He's falling! he's falling! he's falling to his death!

HUBERT (shutting his manuscript on Icarus). Everything happened as was anticipated: my novel is finished.